MURDER AT THE RETREAT

A ROSE BLAIR MURDER MYSTERY

JUDY KEIGHTLEY

COZY HOUSE PRESS

COZY HOUSE PRESS
MAKE A DATE WITH MURDER

An Imprint for GracePoint Publishing (www.GracePointPublishing.com)

GracePoint Matrix, LLC
624 S. Cascade Ave
Suite 201
Colorado Springs, CO 80903
www.GracePointMatrix.com
Email: Admin@GracePointMatrix.com
SAN # 991-6032

ISBN-13: (Paperback) —978-1-951694-58-6
eISBN: (eBook) - 978-1-951694-57-9

Books may be purchased for educational, business, or sales promotional use.
For bulk order requests and price schedule contact:
Orders@GracePointPublishing.com

MAKE A DATE WITH MURDER...

Find Cozy House Press online to read more great cozy mysteries!

www.cozyhousepress.com

COZY HOUSE PRESS
MAKE A DATE WITH MURDER

ACKNOWLEDGMENTS

There are as usual many people to acknowledge in the writing of this, my sixth Rose Blair Murder Mystery novel.

I would like to thank our son Peter for giving me the idea of using a fictitious Mennonite community as a vehicle to move the story along.

I was shocked however after doing the research on the subject, at the relatively high percentage of drug users living in Huron County. This is a real social issue that needs addressing, not only in Huron County but throughout the Province of Ontario.

There are many wonderful people in my life who have listened to me talking about the unfolding plot, murder, and motive for so long that I must apologise for boring the socks off all of you. Thank you for your patience and understanding. In particular, I would like to thank Rita, Alison, and Paulette for reading the manuscript and providing their comments.

My darling husband has also had to put up with my preoccupation whilst writing and my general reluctance to do any cooking or indeed house work during this intense month of writing. I love you for always being there for me.

Finally, I would like to thank NaNoWriMo the online writing support group for budding authors, for providing the incentive to get fifty thousand words written in one month. It really has been an endeavour but is also an excellent way to keep me on track.

I would like to dedicate this book to the Memory of my husband's uncle Daniel Thomas 'Bernie' Moloney who passed away this last year.
Also, in memory of our darling cat Ethan who was taken one strange mystical night by coyotes who came into the village during a full moon. He is missed by all, including our other pets.

PROLOGUE

The young girl with the dark hair and big brown eyes watched from her hideout in the hibiscus bushes that lined the driveway to the estancia. Men in scruffy clothes with head bands tied across their sweaty foreheads, loaded bag after bag of what looked like sugar into the back of the beat up old Land Rover.

Her daddy shouted at them to hurry up as he had a meeting later that evening at the Rotary club and time was money to him, despite the affluence that he obviously enjoyed in his privileged life.

She was about to shout out to her father when a black car came roaring up to the house with a gun man at the wheel firing blindly at the group of men.

At that moment, shots rang out from the garage adjoining the house and the driver suddenly lost control and careened into the bush, only narrowly missing the girl by inches.

She cried out and her father came running over to grab her as the car burst into flames...

ONE

Tom pulled a long face as he flicked through the glossy leaflet in his hand.

"Are you really quite sure that you want to go on this couples retreat love?" He asked Rose who was preoccupied with packing an overnight bag.

"Oh Tom, of course I want to go. Besides, Anne sent it to us as a present, so we have to go. She'll no doubt want to know all about it and besides, I've never been on a couples retreat before. It could be quite good fun."

Tom shook his head. It all sounded so new age. "Freeing Your Inner Child," he read. "Be at One with Your Creativity, Embrace your Sexuality." He just knew that the book *Women are from Venus and Men from Mars* would also be part of the weekend's agenda. He let out a deep sigh. Well at least it was just for one weekend he thought as he picked up his pajamas and stuffed them into the bag.

Rose's friend, Lynda, recently back from West Palm Beach, had promised to take care of Ben and Puff, their beloved dogs, and she arrived just as Rose was putting their overnight bags into Tom's car.

"Perfect timing," Lynda said as she greeted Rose with a warm hug. Ben and Puff, hearing Lynda's voice, came charging out of the house, barking with excitement.

"Oh, you lovely puppies. We're going to have such fun together." Lynda turned to Rose and said, "Is it okay if they spend the weekend at our house? It would be much easier for me."

"Gosh, yes, of course as long as you don't mind all the dog hair!"

Rose had a mental image flash through her mind of Lynda and Barry's immaculate living room with Puff and Ben jumping up on their white sofa and leaving black hairs everywhere.

"Okay, then, let's go." Lynda said taking the dog leashes from Tom who held them out to her, "Have a great weekend away." Lynda waved goodbye and was then dragged off by two exuberant dogs who didn't give either Rose or Tom a second glance.

"Shallow creatures," Tom muttered as he got into his car and waited for Rose to join him.

Ivy Cottage Retreat was nestled down a small lane just past the Ben Miller Inn. The Maitland River meandered slowly alongside the road and shimmered and sparkled under the late May sun. Summer had finally arrived, and green leaves now covered the trees and daffodils nodded their golden heads in the light breeze.

As Rose and Tom pulled up in front of the not-so cottagey looking building, more like an old red brick farm house than anything else, a young woman dressed entirely in black came tripping down the front entrance and waved Tom over to park beneath a clump of maple trees by the side of the house. There were already a few other cars parked neatly side by side under the shade of the trees.

"Are you quite sure that you want to do this, love?" Tom asked as he manoeuvred around the cars already parked and deftly reversed his Audi TT in between a Range Rover and a Ford Escape.

"You really are reluctant to enter into the spirit of this weekend, aren't you? Look, it will be fine, just wait and see, try to keep an open mind."

Tom sighed and nodded his head. This trip was more about Rose and her recovery than anything else. Although, personally a weekend in Toronto would have suited him much better, but he knew that their daughter Anne had the best of intentions. After the trauma of the previous summer when Rose had almost died from a severe head injury, this getaway was supposed to be recuperative as much as anything else.

They entered the farm house building and noticed immediately the calm, Zen-like atmosphere. Tingly music played through unseen speakers. The young woman from the car-park smiled at them and said, "Welcome to Ivy Cottage. Here is the itinerary for this weekend's retreat. If you follow me, I'll show you to your room and you can freshen up before we have our welcome session. It's at 4:00 p.m."

Thank goodness we have our own bathroom, Rose thought as she glanced at the big claw footed bath and anti-quated taps. Their room was at the end of the corridor and inside a four-poster bed fairly dominated the otherwise rather small room. The walls were papered with a rather chintzy flowery pattern and the furniture looked antique and far too heavy for Rose's liking. A tiny washroom with an equally small shower was squeezed into the corner of the room. The space however was light and airy and looked clean and fresh.

Rose bounced on the bed and then lay down. "Come on Tom, stop pulling a face. Just try to be positive. Let's look at the agenda. Um... welcome at 4:00, dinner at 6:00, followed by couple's trivia, and then a meditation before lights out at 10:00 p.m. That doesn't sound too bad, does it?"

Tom had taken his shoes off and was lying next to Rose on the bed contemplating the ceiling. He closed his eyes and tried to imagine that they were in a smart hotel in Toronto and not in the strange farmhouse called Ivy Cottage.

It somehow irked him that the house was called Ivy Cottage when it plainly was a rambling, old farmhouse with absolutely no sign of any ivy anywhere.

"So, Tom, what do you think?" Rose looked at her husband who seemingly had fallen asleep. Her question, however, was never answered as there was a loud knock on their bedroom door.

Rose leapt off the bed and opened it. Standing in her stockinged feet stood an exotically beautiful woman. She was a few inches taller than Rose, but whereas Rose was rather plump and round, this woman was slim and attractively turned out in a tight-fitting navy-blue sheath dress, set off by a huge oval opal pendant with matching earrings.

Her thick, chestnut brown hair cascaded in curls down to her shoulders and her creamy beige skin glowed with good health. Her lips were painted bright red, which on another woman might have looked cheap, but on her it served only to accentuate the fullness of her sensual lips. She was a beautiful woman and for a moment Rose felt a pang of jealousy envelope her.

"Can I help you?" Rose enquired wondering just who the apparition was and what she was doing knocking on their door.

"I was just wondering where the welcome was to take place? Oh, by the way," she said, holding out an elegantly manicured hand, "my name is Juliet. I do hope that I didn't wake you." Rose noticed her glancing over at a sleepy looking Tom now sitting up on the bed.

Rose took her hand which was surprisingly cool and soft.

"Oh, no, we weren't sleeping. My name is Rose, and this is my husband, Tom. You know, in answer to your question I'm not sure where the welcome session will be. I would imagine that it would be in the living room. We haven't checked out the facilities here yet. It's a bit strange being called a cottage though when it clearly is a farmhouse, isn't it?"

Juliet smiled and answered, "Ah ha, now that is something I can explain to you. If you look outside your bedroom window, you'll see a little foot path. It leads to the sweetest log cabin which is all covered in ivy. Presumably that's the original Ivy Cottage."

"Gosh, how did you discover that?"

"Oh, Harry and I arrived here hours ago and explored the grounds and the house. It's all been a bit weird as nobody seemed to be around until a young woman dressed in black appeared and showed us to our room. I've been waiting for someone else to arrive for ages as I was beginning to feel some-what apprehensive with just the two of us in this creepy, old building."

As Juliet was talking, Rose overheard footsteps in the hall as another couple was shown to their room. Rose looked at her watch. It was only 2:45 p.m., they still had over an hour to go before their welcome session.

I could kill for a cup of tea, she thought, as Juliet left to go back to her room and Rose closed the door.

"Tom, do you mind if I go and explore? I'll see if I can find a place to get us both a nice cup of tea. I won't be long." She bent over and gave Tom a quick kiss on his cheek and left the room quietly.

Walking back down the hallway, Rose overheard voices coming from several of the neighbouring bedrooms. The other couples' retreat guests were finally arriving.

Downstairs however, was still very quiet apart from the tingly sound of music. Rose walked to the back of the house rationalizing that kitchens generally were found not in the front of old homes but normally hidden away at the back. Sure enough, a small, galley-like kitchen was annexed to the side of a very large dining room.

Rose stepped in and immediately spied a kettle. *Now for the tea and cups,* she thought, opening and closing cupboards in her quest for a cup of tea. She had just spotted a box of tea bags when the sound of raised voices caught her attention and Rose immediately recognized Juliet's husky voice.

"Stop being so possessive Harry. I told you that I only met him for one drink. You know that James and I go back years. He's one of my oldest friends from university, plus the fact that he's happily married. Can't I have my own friends, now?"

Rose held her breath as she listened to the angry response, presumably from Harry, Juliet's husband.

"I just don't trust you, Julie. After your past behaviour, do you truly blame me? Look, if you want a divorce I'll give you one. I can't take the lies and deceit anymore, that's all."

"Oh, Harry, why do you think that I booked this couples retreat for us. I love you. I only wish you could understand that!"

Rose didn't hear any more of the conversation as suddenly the young woman who had greeted them popped her head around the door and said in a rather steely voice, "Can I help you?"

Rose almost jumped out of her skin, "Oh... yes, well, I really would love a cup of tea."

"Refreshments are in the living room," the woman said, clearly peeved to find Rose poking around the kitchen. "It's this way," and she pointed back to the front of the house. Rose followed her directions, turning as she left the hall to try to see where Juliet and her husband had been having their heated discussion.

The living room was at the front of the house and it was quite delightful. A large room with a stone fireplace opened out onto a beautiful sun lounge. There were colourful scatter cushions and bean bags on the carpeted floor as well as several comfortable arm chairs.

In the corner of the room a table had been set up with flasks of coffee, tea, and juice, along with plates of banana loaf and butter tarts with side plates and colourful serviettes. Newspapers and magazines were fanned out on a coffee table.

It all looked well organized. It would be much nicer having tea in the living room rather than up in their bedroom, thought Rose as she turned to go and get Tom.

TWO

Rose returned to their room only to find Tom fast asleep. Rather than wake him, she closed the door quietly and went back down stairs to the living room. Pouring herself out a cup of tea and helping herself to a piece of the scrumptious banana loaf, Rose sat on one of the comfy armchairs and started to feel herself relax. She was determined to enjoy this weekend getaway come what may.

By four o'clock the other guests began to trickle into the living room. Tom appeared looking a little dishevelled and made a beeline for the tea. Looking around the room Rose noticed that the other couples varied in ages from one thirty-something couple to several around Rose and Tom's ages.

Rose suddenly realized that she and Tom knew one of the couples, Karen and Brian Huber, who were fellow members of the Bayfield International Croquet Club.

They were standing in the corner looking decidedly uncomfortable. Rose really liked Karen. She didn't know her very well but had often chatted with her whilst playing at the croquet courts and during the Thursday evening cocktail parties.

The Croquet Club season had not yet begun, and she knew that the Huber's were snowbirds disappearing off to Barbados every January. She rarely saw them during the winter or spring, so it was a big surprise seeing them together at the couple's retreat. Everyone looked a bit apprehensive as nobody knew quite what to expect from the retreat.

Suddenly their hosts, a man and a woman both dressed in black, appeared and the background noise of polite chatter stopped, leaving the room strangely silent.

The man looked around at the assembled couples commanding their attention. He was of average height with a silvery grey goatee and the most arresting blue eyes. He reminded Rose of the actor Terence Stamp and she found herself quite attracted to him.

His partner was also quite eye catching and dramatic with her long braided blonde hair and elfin-like features. She smiled broadly and said "Welcome, welcome everyone, please follow us" whilst directing everyone into the adjacent sunroom.

The couple, who still hadn't introduced themselves, asked all the women to form a circle in the centre of the room facing outwards and then directed the men to make an outer circle facing the women. They all followed their directions like school children being instructed by their class teacher.

Rose found herself standing opposite Harry, Juliet's husband.

"Right, now, I want you to look deeply and intently into the eyes of the person you are facing for one minute and just say your name. When I say move, just the men in the outer circle will move clockwise around to face the next woman in the circle. Remember everyone that your eyes are the window to your souls."

Rose daren't catch Tom's eyes for fear of giggling. Time enough when it would be their turn to face each other. She obeyed their instructor and turned her attention to Harry.

Looking into someone else's eyes proved oddly satisfying. Rose felt that she could see Harry's pain. The longer that she peered into his sage green eyes the more angst she could feel. *Am I just projecting what I overheard in the kitchen,* Rose thought, as she studied the man's features while still trying to remain eye locked.

"Now can the men only move to the left," commanded their instructor, and Harry moved away, leaving Rose to face none other than Brian Huber.

"Hi," Rose whispered to a rather embarrassed looking Brian. They eye-locked, but this time Rose couldn't stay focused. She knew Brian and it felt decidedly awkward looking into a familiar face.

Next it was Tom, and they both tried to suppress giggles as they stared at each other and tried to look into each other's souls. Rose just knew what Tom would be thinking. Poor Tom, he just hated all the new-age stuff.

After engaging in the exercise with the two other men, Jerry and Mike, as well as the facilitator who revealed to Rose that he was called Seb, the exercise was over and Seb and his partner gathered the group all around them.

"Now that you have introduced yourselves let me intro-duce Sonja and myself. My name is Dr. Sebastian Miller, but you can call me Seb for short, and this is Sonja my wife. We are both qualified sex therapists and we ask that you trust the process and keep an open mind. Before dinner we will be having couple's trivia, a getting-to-know-you quiz, but before that we're going to do a short exercise in trust."

Sonja produced a bag full of coloured scarves and started to hand them out.

"Now, I want you to blindfold your partner, making sure there is no peeping, and then the blindfolded partner must fall forward and be caught in your partner's arms. Okay, decide which of you will go first."

Tom looked at Rose and smiled saying, "Right, off you go and blindfold me. I trust in you explicitly."

Rose looked at Tom and said, "Well, I hope that I can catch you, you're awfully heavy." She blindfolded Tom and stood about three feet in front of him copying what other couples were doing. She glanced over at Karen and caught her eye and raised her eyebrows.

"Right, Tom, fall forward into my arms."

Tom stood there blindfolded and hesitated. "Are you quite sure that you're going to catch me, love?"

"Yes, Tom, of course I'll catch you. Just do it."

Tom let out a deep sigh and forced himself to fall forward into Rose's open arms.

"There, you did it, well done, Tom."

Tom took the blindfold off and handed it to Rose, "Your turn next, love. It's not as easy as it looks."

Rose soon understood what Tom had meant. It really was a test of trust. *I wonder how Juliet and Harry are getting on*, Rose thought as she felt herself falling and hoping above all hopes that Tom would be there to catch her, which of course, he was.

"Now this is our last exercise before dinner everyone and it's the Couple's Trivia – How well do you know each other. Sonja will be handing out the quiz sheets and some pens. I want you to find a quiet place and answer the questions with total honesty. I will give you ten minutes and then you will exchange quiz sheets with your partner. Right, off you all go and remember, you must be totally honest with your answers."

Rose and Tom took themselves off to the living room and grabbed two comfortable armchairs before anyone else could. Neither of them fancied sitting on the floor cushions or the bean bags in the sun room.

Rose scanned the quiz in front of her. Most of the questions were multiple choice.

1. Does your partner snore; (a) - sometimes, (b) - never, (c) - like a train
2. How often does your partner say I love you; (a) - once a week, (b) - more than once a week, (c) – never.

And so, the questions went on.

After ten minutes Seb Miller rang a bell and told everyone to exchange their quiz sheets. Tom rather sheepishly handed Rose his sheet. "Don't be offended, love. Seb told us to be honest."

Rose glanced at Tom's answers to the quiz. The first thing she noticed was that he had her down as snoring like a train. *I don't snore,* she thought indignantly, and then glanced at the second question and her bristles spiked up again. *I never declare my love, oh, how dare Tom say that* Rose thought, and so it went on so that by the end of reading the quiz Rose felt somewhat dejected and thoroughly miserable. The trouble was, in truth, everything that Tom had said was correct and she suddenly felt thoroughly ashamed of herself. How could she have taken Tom for granted all these years? He was such a good man and she really did love him. *I must tell him just how*

I feel, she thought, as she looked over to where Tom was frowning.

They didn't have time for further accusations because Seb rang the bell again and called out that dinner was being served. Rose glanced around the room and noticed Juliet and Harry both wearing thunderous faces. *Gosh, if looks could kill those two would be dead,* Rose thought as she followed Tom into the dining room.

Candles were lit and the ambiance was very romantic. Although the dining table was set out family style with dishes of delicious looking food to be passed around, everything looked very elegant. Karen and Brian sat next to Tom and Rose and they were finally able to talk to each other for the first time since arriving.

"So, Karen, Brian, what are you doing here?" Rose said whilst quickly adding, "You might ask us the very same question, but you go first."

Karen smiled, "Well, actually Brian and I were the winning bidders for this retreat at the Croquet Club's silent auction last July. Apparently, the owner of Ivy Cottage is Margo's cousin and she kindly donated this weekend. So, what about you and Tom, what are you doing here?"

"Oh, that's easy. Anne, our daughter from Halifax, gave it to us as a Christmas present. We didn't want to come in the winter, so we waited until Spring and here we are."

Dinner was served and an excellent meal it turned out to be. The first course was cod au gratin served in individual terracotta dishes. This was followed by beef stroganoff served on a bed of jasmine rice with snow peas and julienne carrots. Dessert was stewed pears poached in red wine served with maple ice cream. A cheese board was passed around. Rose noticed that no alcohol was served which was fine by her, but she wondered what the other guests might think. As if reading her mind, Seb stood up and clinked his water glass with his fork.

"Ladies and gentlemen, once again, welcome to Ivy Cottage. You will notice that no alcohol has been served and that was on purpose. This weekend is all about discovering who you really are, and alcohol will most certainly alter the real you. Tonight, we will have an early to bed curfew after our peace-filled meditation. Now eat up and enjoy the rest of the evening. Tomorrow will be a busy day."

They sat enjoying their meal a while longer and then made their way into the sun room where the blinds had been drawn and lights turned down low. The ubiquitous tinkly music was playing softly in the background and candles flickered and cast shadows on the wall. Everyone was quiet and waited for their instructions.

Seb entered the room and commanded their attention once again. "With your partner I want you to sit on the floor facing each other. Put your hands up and just touch each other's fingers lightly. Close your eyes and feel the love move into your fingertips. Remember to clear your mind of any thoughts other than the love that you feel for each other."

It was all very well Seb telling them to sit on the floor, Rose thought. Sitting was one thing but getting up off the floor was quite another. *Oh, well*, she thought, *I suppose Tom can always heave me up.*

Funnily enough, Rose and Tom quite enjoyed the meditation and by the time it was bed time they were both feeling quite romantic. It was only nine o'clock when they turned out the light which is why at two o'clock in the morning Rose sat bolt upright, wide awake. She had been woken by a noise and she felt disoriented and confused waking up in a strange bed, in a strange farm house.

Quietly getting out of bed she padded over to the window and looked outside. There was a moonlit sky so it was easy to spot what looked like Juliet walking down the drive with a man whom, from a distance, did not look at all like Harry.

Where on earth would she be going at two in the morning Rose thought as she went to the toilet and padded back to bed. She was soon sound asleep and by day break had pushed the incident into the deep recesses of her mind.

THREE

SATURDAY

Breakfast was a relaxed affair laid out in the dining room. Tom and Rose noticed that three other couples including Karen and Brian were already seated chatting to each other and looking well rested, except for Harry who was sitting on his own. He got up as Rose and Tom walked in and approached them asking, "Have you seen my wife Juliet at all this morning?"

Harry continued rather gruffly, "It appears that she's gone for a walk about. She must have left before I even woke up this morning."

Even then Rose didn't recall what she had seen in the middle of the night. In fact, it all had taken on a dream quality. "Well, that's where she is then," Rose suggested, "She'll be back soon, I'm sure."

"I hope so. We're leaving this cuckoo place just as soon as she returns. I can't wait to get out of here." With that he turned his back on them and walked out of the dining room.

"What a miserable sod," Tom said quietly to Rose.

After breakfast Seb rang his bell and asked everyone to go through to the living room and then gathered the group around him. Sonja entered carrying a large, wicker box containing, as it was soon revealed, hats, wigs, boas, and all sorts of theatrical costumes.

"Now, ladies and gentlemen, you are going to entertain us by recreating a remarkable event or events that have taken place during your marriage.

You have thirty minutes to put together your little skit and performances will start at 10:30 in the sun room. Help yourselves to costumes and props and remember to keep it positive and light and to have fun."

Rose and Tom collected together an assortment of hats and wigs from the box and once again commandeered the comfy armchairs.

"So, Tom, where do we start?"

They didn't get very far before being interrupted by a commotion in the hall. Voices, loud voices, could be heard and they both recognized Harry's voice. He was obviously on a rampage.

"I tell you, my wife's gone missing. I've looked everywhere and she's not here."

It was then that Rose remembered looking out of the window in the early hours of the morning and seeing Juliet walking down the drive. "Tom, I thought I saw her last night outside with a man. I should tell Harry."

She got up and walked into the hall where Harry was pacing up and down like a caged lion while berating the young woman, Rose still didn't know her name, who was trying valiantly to calm him down.

"Excuse me, Harry, I've just remembered something. I

think that I saw Juliet walking down the driveway in the middle of the night. Umm... she was with a man."

Harry turned on Rose and shouted at her. "Well why the hell didn't you tell me this at breakfast?"

"I hadn't remembered then," Rose stumbled, "I mean I wasn't expecting to see anyone outside in the middle of the night and I thought that maybe I'd been dreaming."

"You stupid woman," Harry said, "I demand that we call together a search party and let's have every inch of this place turned over inside and out. She might have fallen and knocked herself out, got lost, trapped, or something."

"Tom and I will start by searching the grounds outside," Rose said rather taken aback by his manner, and went off to fetch Tom.

They started off by walking down the driveway where Rose had last seen Juliet. The drive led to the road and gave up no clues as to her whereabouts.

"Let's go down through the trees over by that pathway. Didn't Juliet say that the real Ivy Cottage was through there?" Rose said, pointing over to where their cars were parked under a clump of trees. A small pathway cut its way through the trees and disappeared into the woods. They walked through the trees until they came upon a log cabin absolutely covered in ivy.

"This just has to be the original Ivy Cottage," Tom said.

"It looks pretty over grown although look, Tom, the front door is slightly open."

"Well, what are we waiting for, love, let's have a look." Tom pushed the door ajar and walked in, followed tentatively by Rose.

Looking into the gloom they immediately noticed an over

turned chair and a wooden table. As their eyes adjusted to the darkness they could see a body sprawled out on the dusty wooden floor. Rose and Tom knew straight away that they had found Juliet and it was not a pretty sight.

FOUR

etective Chief Inspector Susan Parker was enjoying a quiet weekend on her own when the telephone rang. It was the Serious Crimes Unit in London. As Susan listened to the dispatch officer relating the details of a suspicious death she rolled her eyes and sighed. Gone was her relaxed weekend, death waited for no one.

She looked at her watch. It was just after 10:30 in the morning and she wondered if she should call in the SOC team now or wait until she had surveyed the scene of the suspicious death herself.

And, of course, if it was determined to be a murder then she would have to set up the investigation unit which, likely, would be based yet again out of the Lion's Hall in Bayfield.

Yet the crime scene was close to Ben Miller, Susan thought, and she did recall that there was a community hall there which she might be able to commandeer for the duration of the inquiry.

I'm jumping the gun, Susan thought to herself as she changed from her sloppy jeans and sweatshirt into what she called her professional wardrobe, which in this case was a navy blue pair of pants with a turquoise blue silk shirt and jacket.

She was ready in ten minutes and walked outside her Harbour Lights condo to where her new Porsche 718 Boxter was parked. This was Susan's latest indulgence, bought on the spur of the moment after Peter, her boyfriend, had announced that he was joining the National Geographic Photographic team to film penguins in Antarctica, and he would be away for ten months.

Feeling incredibly sorry for herself, Susan had fallen in love with the metallic silver Porsche and had never looked back. She adored the sense of freedom she felt when driving the Porsche as it growled along the sleepy roads of Huron County.

SUSAN REACHED Ivy Cottage fifteen minutes after she had left home and immediately noticed Tom's Audi TT parked under the trees at the side of the farm house. What were her good friends Tom and Rose doing here, she thought as she got out of her car and walked towards the farm house.

Once inside she could hear music and laughter, not the normal sounds associated with death. A young woman dressed all in black appeared and beckoned Susan to follow her outside.

"Come this way. Are you the Police?" She whispered.

Stranger and stranger, Susan thought as she followed the woman outside.

"Look, what's going on here?" she said. "I got a call to say that a body had been found. I sincerely hope that nobody is wasting my time here!"

"No, no, ma'am," she stumbled, "by the way, I'm Lydia and there is a body I can assure you, follow me."

Susan followed Lydia, passing the collection of cars parked beneath the trees and down a small path which took them into a small wood. There in a clearing Susan saw a rustic log cabin covered in ivy and standing outside was Rose, Tom, and another man, who held his head in his hands and appeared to be sobbing.

Rose looked up and saw Susan coming down the pathway. "Thank goodness you've come. He's totally inconsolable. He's been sobbing and wailing for twenty minutes now."

Susan looked at her normally composed friend Rose and could see stress written all over her face. Tom also looked suitably crushed and between them both they looked to have aged and grown haggard overnight.

"So, what exactly do we have here?" Susan said as she pulled out a pair of latex gloves preparing to put them on.

"Umm... inside that building is the body. It's Juliet Carmichael, that man's wife."

Rose proceeded to relay to Susan their story, concluding with the fact that no one else on the couples retreat actually knew about the murder yet, and the management wanted to keep it that way for as long as possible.

"Okay, I want you and Tom to go back to the house and I'll take it from here. You both look as if you could do with a rest. It's been a nasty shock for you. I'll speak to you both later."

Tom and Rose nodded and quietly walked back to the farmhouse while Susan went inside the cabin.

Juliet was lying face down on the floor. By the angle of her head in relation to her body, it was obvious that her neck had been broken. There was no sign of blood or indeed of any flesh wounds.

Forensics would have to determine if she had been raped but from a preliminary examination of the body there was no obvious indication of recent sexual activity. In fact, she was wearing only a t-shirt style night gown and her feet were clad in sheep skin slippers.

From what Susan could see she appeared to have been an attractive woman probably in her forties. By the angle of her neck and the way she was lying this certainly did not look like the result of an accidental death. Susan reached for her phone to call in the troops. She would also have to set up an incident room as soon as possible and pull together her team.

So much for a quiet weekend, she thought as she went outside to talk to the grieving husband.

AS IT TURNED out the Ben Miller Community Hall was closed for renovations. It would have to be the Lion's Hall in Bayfield. Susan knew the President of the Lion's Club and in the past, he had bent over backwards to help.

He was an amazing man and, if it wasn't for his adoring wife, Susan could have quite fancied him. She made her phone call and nodded in approval when she had his consent to use the hall.

Next on her list was to phone up her team. Sergeant Flowers, Constables Brown and Elliot, and her rooky Constable Ryan. The previous year they had worked supremely well as a team when they had uncovered a serial killer in the village of Bayfield.

Two authors attending a Literary Festival held at The Little Inn had been murdered. It had proven to be a challenging case, but her team had worked tirelessly and had the case cracked within a week.

She would also have to call in the police photographer, the new photographer who had replaced her boyfriend, Peter Joyce. She hadn't worked with him before and, indeed, had not even met the man.

Forensics would also have to be contacted and Susan wondered whether the forensics officer, Ian from Goderich, would be called in or whether their London officer would be dispatched. She secretly hoped that it would be Dr. Ian Green, as she had enjoyed getting to know him quite a bit the previous summer.

With all the formalities and necessary calls dealt with, Susan turned to the victim's husband, Harry who had joined her while she was making her phone calls and who looked quite distraught.

"Right, sir, I need to have a word with you" she said, steering him gently away from the cabin. "Let's go back to the house. I noticed a bench under a gazebo in the garden. How about I bring out a cup of coffee and you can tell me all about it."

Harry was a good-looking man in a rugged sort of way. His brown hair was worn unfashionably long, and his clothes looked expensive but somewhat retro. His eyes, however, were what drew Susan's attention and set off alarm bells.

She had seen eyes like his many times before and she didn't trust them. The term shifty came to mind, but there was something even deeper, more animalistic than just plain shiftiness. There was an arrogance and an air of entitlement that flitted in and out between the wracks of sobs.

Susan handed over a strong cup of coffee having asked Lydia to fetch it from the house. She sat down next to him on the bench and opened up her iPad ready for questioning.

"So, Harry, when did you last see your wife?"

"Last night, after the meditation we retired to our room. We went to bed early about nine and when I awoke the next morning she was gone." Fresh sobs started to shake his body.

Susan paused a minute giving Harry time to compose himself before continuing, "What sort of mood was your wife in before you went to bed?"

Harry turned to look at Susan and fairly shouted at her. "What sort of question do you think that is? We both hated this weekend, couldn't wait to leave, so no, we were not in good spirits. In fact, we both were in absolutely foul moods if you really want to know."

"What about your marriage. Were you happily married?"

"Now how am I meant to answer that?" Harry growled, "We had our ups and downs, but on a whole we were reasonably happy."

Susan was spared any more questioning as the SOC team had arrived and started cordoning off the area with yellow tape. Then the police photographer arrived and introduced himself to Susan. He was a young man probably still only in his twenties, wet behind the ears and in all likelihood green behind the gills. His name was Jack Ross.

"Straight through to the cabin," Susan said, and pointed Jack in the right direction. "Um. the SOC team are busy in there, you might want to boot up out here." Susan was referring to the white SOC overalls and booties worn at all crime scenes, although she herself had not donned any garments before entering the scene of crime, just her latex gloves.

IAN ARRIVED ALREADY DRESSED in his whites, latex gloves on, and his suitcase in his hand. Susan looked up and waved to him, "Hi, Ian, long time no see. How are you?" She smiled at him and suddenly felt all warm and fuzzy. Yes, she definitely liked him, a lot. She wondered if his mother was still going strong and whether he was still living at home helping with the chicken farm.

Ian ambled over, "Susan, good to see you again. We must stop meeting like this," he laughed. "So, who do we have here then?" He looked over at Harry, "It's not you, Harry Carmichael, is it?"

Harry looked up and for once his eyes lost their shiftiness as recognition glimmered. "Oh, it's you, Ian. My curling partner," he added gesturing at Ian as he turned to Susan for explanation. Ian started to respond to Harry then then stopped short as he realised the significance of Susan interviewing his buddy and the fact that there was a body to examine.

Ian had only met the lovely Juliet on one occasion and that was at a curling party and she had come over as somewhat flirtatious. He hoped that it wasn't her in the cabin, but he had an awful sinking feeling that his deduction might be right.

"I'll go and have a look then," Ian said, waving his hand at Susan and heading in the direction of the yellow tape and the SOC team.

Before Susan could continue her conversation with Harry her phone rang. It was Sergeant Flowers saying that he was available and just awaiting instructions. He had also spoken to the other three young Constables and all of them were available and willing to join the investigation.

Susan smiled and turned to the grieving husband saying, "Okay, Harry, where were we?"

FIVE

Tom and Rose sat quietly on their bed in their small, farm house bedroom.

"I think that I want to go home, Tom." Rose said in a small voice.

"Yes, me too," replied Tom.

They stood up together and started to pack, neither of them saying a single word.

Back on the road again after checking out, Tom finally spoke. "Look, love, we'll have another weekend away soon, I promise. Where do you fancy going?"

Rose contemplated a few options. "I don't think that I actually want to go away anywhere for a while, Tom. But maybe next time we could go and check out the wineries in Prince Edward County or Pelee Island.

Actually, I enjoyed last night, and I realize now how I've been neglecting you. You do know how much I adore you, don't you, Tom?"

Tom chuckled. "Of course I do my love. Look, we wouldn't

still be together after 45 years if there wasn't still some spark left between us."

"So, we'll thank Anne for sending us away on a couples retreat. If nothing else, it's reinforced our love for each other. But Tom, I can't stop thinking about Juliet and her husband Harry. What do you think, did he murder her?"

"Well, if he did, he's a bloody good actor." Tom said, "all that sobbing, and woe is me. No, I don't think he killed her. My guess is that it was that mysterious man that you saw her walking with, otherwise who else would be out and about at two in the morning?"

Rose was quiet for a while and deep in thought. "Could she have arranged to meet him there? Maybe she was having an affair?"

Tom stopped Rose sharply, "Rose you are not going to get involved. Promise me that you will not snoop into this murder case."

"But Tom, we are already involved by the sheer fact that we discovered the body. But I doubt if I'll be able to find out anything else unless Susan slips some vital information."

Tom couldn't see the gleam in Rose's eyes as he was too intent on driving back to Bayfield, but if he had he would have noticed a definite spark lighting up her eyes.

THEY ARRIVED home shortly after lunch. Neither of them was hungry and so they went straight inside their charming house and Rose put the kettle on while Tom made a beeline for the bedroom.

"Where are you going, Tom?" Rose said, "I was just making us a cup of tea."

"I'm going to bed, love. I don't feel like any tea. Don't let anyone know that we're back. I'd like to lay low for a day or two. That murder has knocked the stuffing out of me."

Rose looked concerned. Poor Tom. He had really seemed quite shocked to find the dead body of Juliet Carmichael. He was a sensitive soul and one prone to depression. She would have to be gentle with him.

Having boiled the kettle, Rose made herself a cup of tea and took it into the sun room. The house did seem quiet without Puff and Ben, yet it felt strangely okay not having them around to fuss and play.

Those eyes of Harry's, Rose thought. There was definitely something about his eyes that troubled her. As for Juliet, remembering the overheard conversation and the inference that she was seeing another man called James, possibly conducting an affair with him, could cause the oldest crime in the world to have ensued, that of a crime of passion.

If Harry truly had found out that Juliet was having an adulterous affair, then he would have a motive for murder. According to their conversation he had his strong suspicions but no real proof and, of course, Juliet had denied it.

Oh, I must stop thinking about it, Rose thought as she felt a bad headache come on. The doctor had warned her about getting too stressed out. Since her severe head injury, she had experienced all kinds of post concussion symptoms. Blurred vision, dizziness, memory loss, and blinding headaches, all emphasized when she was either tired or stressed.

Maybe I'll just go and lie down with Tom, she thought, and swallowed her tea quickly before going into the bedroom only to find Tom sound asleep. She kicked off her shoes and climbed under the duvet and soon was fast asleep too.

SIX

Susan drove back to Bayfield deep in thought. For once the joy of driving her new Porsche failed to take over her as her mind was on overdrive thinking about the murder.

Since moving to the sleepy village of Bayfield there had been an inordinate number of murders. Everyone made fun of her at the Serious Crimes Squad in London saying that Bayfield had to be the murder capital of Ontario, and it was true.

There had been five murders in so many years, quite unbelievable really, considering the demographics of the village. The other unfathomable fact was that her friend, Rose Blair had also been like a magnet for the murders. In one way or another she had helped solve each one of those cases.

Uncanny and decidedly weird, Susan thought as she pulled into the Lion's Hall car park. It was two o'clock and she had arranged for her team to convene at three. *I think that I'll pop over and do my formal interview with Rose and Tom,* Susan thought, and that way she would have some first-hand notes to share with her team.

Driving down Main Street Susan noticed that the tourist season had already begun. After Victoria Day weekend everything came to life in the village and this year there had been a few changes in the streetscape.

Da Vinci's was gone and replaced with the Bayfield Pub, and a few other shops had closed, and new ones opened. It was like a game of musical chairs and always amused the locals.

Susan turned right down Catherine Street and continued on to Bayfield Terrace where Rose and Tom lived. She knocked on their door and instead of being greeted effusively by Ben and Puff, the Blair's beloved dogs, a sleepy looking Rose answered.

"Oh, Rose, sorry, did I wake you?" Susan said feeling bad that she had obviously disturbed the Blair household.

"Oh, no, come on in. Tom is asleep, but I'll make us a cup of tea and we can talk. I'm sorry that we rushed away from Ivy Cottage. I knew that you would understand, you see Tom felt overwhelmed by the whole ghastliness of the murder."

If it had been anyone other than the Blair's, Susan would have admonished them for leaving a scene of crime, but Susan just smiled and told Rose that it was all fine. She did, however, have to interview both Tom and her.

"Well, I'm actually glad that you stopped by as I've got much to tell you starting with my seeing Juliet outside at two o'clock in the morning. She was with a man."

Susan interrupted her friend sharply. "A man, do you mean Harry or was it someone else?"

Rose continued saying, "No, I don't think that it was Juliet's husband. It was a moonlit night and I just saw the two of them walking down the drive together with their backs to the house. Maybe it was his height, I honestly don't know Susan. It's just that at the time my brain registered that it was not Harry. Sorry to be so vague."

Susan typed away on her iPad before saying, "Are you absolutely sure that it was two in the morning, Rose?"

"Yes, because I went to the toilet and looked at my watch, but that isn't all I've got to tell you." Rose then relayed having overheard Harry and Juliet's argument when she was in the kitchen, concluding with the evening's activities and how neither of them appeared to be enjoying themselves.

"They were obviously having marital problems," Rose said, just as Tom appeared stretching his arms out while yawning at the same time.

"Hello, Susan, when did you get here?"

Susan smiled and told Tom that his was perfect timing as she wanted to ask him a few questions.

"Fire away," Tom said.

"Well, Rose has mentioned that the Carmichaels appeared unhappy. Would you agree?"

Tom thought for a moment and then said, "There was an exercise we did as an introduction to each other. We had to look into each other's eyes. When I conducted this exercise with Juliet I know that it sounds weird, but I could almost feel her pain and sadness. It was really quite palpable."

Tom coughed and cleared his throat. Susan could see that he was visibly moved. "Rose, maybe you could make us that cup of tea that you mentioned?"

Rose nodded and got up and walked to the kitchen leaving Susan alone with Tom.

Susan put her hand on Tom's shoulder as she said, "Tom, you seem really choked up over Juliet's death. Is there anything else you would like to tell me?"

Tom blew his nose hard and looked up at Susan.

"It's just that she was a beautiful, beautiful woman and I felt that she was pleading for my help and I somehow failed her. I know that it sounds absurd, I barely knew the woman, but looking deeply into someone's eyes really is like looking into their souls. It has really quite upset me."

He is a sensitive man, Susan thought. He obviously has been hit badly by Juliet's death.

"You cannot blame yourself, Tom. How were you to know that she would be murdered? No, we will find out who did this, and justice will prevail."

Rose returned carrying a tray holding mugs of steaming tea and a plate of scones. "There you both are, dig in."

Susan took a scone and a small mug of tea saying she really had to leave shortly as her team would be arriving at The Lion's Hall. "If there is anything else that you remember pertinent to this inquiry don't hesitate to call," Susan said as she left Rose and Tom.

SEVEN

Arriving at The Lion's Hall she was pleased to see her team assembled outside waiting for her.

"Welcome, welcome everyone," Susan said as she opened the door and walked into the now familiar room. The Lion's Hall used to be Bayfield's village school and as such the incident room was once a classroom with a chalkboard still in place against one side of the wall.

"Good, you've all brought your iPads or laptops. We're not going to use a display incident board as everything will be kept securely online. We're going paperless. Now, if you go to this portal," here Susan chalked the web site on the board, "Right, click on this site and enter your passwords at login and you should see the preliminary photographs uploaded from the scene of the crime. Any initial observations?"

Constable Holly Ryan put her hand up. She was their rooky Constable and an IT specialist.

"Yes, Holly, what do you observe?"

"Well, ma'am, the body is lying at an unnatural angle. Her head is twisted at more than 90 degrees by the looks of things."

"Good observations, Constable. Anyone else see anything unusual?"

Sergeant Flowers put his hand up to speak.

"Yes, Sergeant, speak up." Susan said. Her Sergeant lacked confidence and she really wished that he would be more assertive.

"Well, ma'am, she appears to be wearing what looks like a night shirt and slippers on her feet."

Susan hadn't noticed the slippers although she had observed that the victim was wearing a night shirt, which made perfect sense if what Rose had said was true, Juliet must have crept out of the house in her night clothes to meet up with the man Rose had seen her with.

"Any more observations?" Susan said.

Constable Elliot put up his hand.

"The room looks as if there's been a struggle. The chairs are overturned, and the table is on its side."

Another good observation, Susan thought as she prepared to fill her team in as to the facts of the case such as they already knew them.

"Okay, here we have the victim, Juliet Carmichael, aged forty-four, married to Harry Carmichael. They live in Exeter, but both work in Goderich. Juliet was a nurse at the Alexandra Marine and General Hospital in Goderich and her husband is an accountant working for Albright and Son on the Square.

"They have no children, and the deceased has no living relatives as both her mother and father died ten years ago in a car accident. She has no siblings. We are waiting the forensic report, but the initial cause of death appears to be from a broken neck, however not due to strangulation.

"The approximate time of death, there again to be confirmed when we receive the full forensics report, is estimated at between 2 a.m., when she was last seen alive, and 3 a.m. this morning. Any questions?"

Holly put her hand up.

"Yes, Constable."

"What was the victim doing at Ivy Cottage, ma'am?"

"Good question, Constable. Ivy Cottage is used as a retreat centre. Dr. Miller conducts two couples retreats a month taking up to six couples. The farmhouse can sleep up to eight couples. To answer your question, Juliet and Harry Carmichael were on the couple's retreat. Okay, so moving on. As you can see by my report, Rose and Tom Blair found the body at 10 a.m. this morning,"

Holly put her hand up again. Susan hated being interrupted. She said impatiently, "What is it now, Constable?"

"Ma'am, you said that it was Rose and Tom Blair who discovered the body. Is that the same Rose Blair we dealt with last year regarding the murders at The Little Inn?"

Susan nodded, though not quite seeing the relevance of this to their case.

"Yes, the Blair's are good friends of mine. You'll be pleased to know that Rose has made a good recovery from her ordeal last year."

Holly looked puzzled. "But, ma'am, what on earth were the Blair's doing at the scene of the crime?"

"Well, that's simple, Constable. They were attending the couple's retreat. In fact, Rose is a key witness and is possibly the last person to have seen Juliet alive."

Susan continued telling the team about the stranger Rose had seen with Juliet outside in the middle of the night.

Holly put her hand up again. "Ma'am, the murderer surely would have been the last person to have seen her alive."

Susan wanted to kick her Constable, but instead she

ground her teeth together and calmly said, "Yes, well, Constable, you state the obvious," Here Susan couldn't help herself, she raised her voice a notch, "Of course the murderer was the last person to see her alive. Now can we please move on."

Constable Ryan pursed her lips and sat there suitably chastised.

"The Blair's found the body after Harry Carmichael initiated a search for his missing wife. They are not on my list of suspects, as they were both in their room having gone back to sleep at the time the murder took place. They are just very valuable witnesses based on what Rose saw. Right, Sergeant Flowers, I would like you to interview the husband, Harry Carmichael. Although I have questioned him already, he needs to be put under the microscope. Leave no stone unturned. Just remember that eighty five percent of cases of spousal murder are crimes of passion. Presently Harry Carmichael is our prime suspect. Constables Brown and Elliot, you need to interview all the couples attending the retreat. I will interview the facilitators, Dr. Miller his wife, Sonya, and their assistant, Lydia. Constable Ryan, I would like you to speak to all of Juliet's friends and business acquaintances. Let's try to get a complete picture of the deceased. Okay, we'll meet back here the same time tomorrow. Any questions?"

Susan looked around the room. She could see that Holly was biting her lip and she felt a tiny bit bad for almost shouting at her. As the rest of the team traipsed out of the room, Susan called Holly over.

"Constable, I just wanted to apologize for raising my voice to you. Now go to it and bring back some results."

Constable Ryan smiled and the tension in the room was released.

EIGHT

Rose was just putting a chicken casserole into the oven when the phone rang. It was their daughter Jessica.

"Hi, Mom. I was wondering if we could come over next Saturday?"

Rose grabbed her planner and had a quick look. They were supposed to be playing Croquet with the Hubers, but that could wait.

"Yes, that would be lovely, dear. How are the girls?"

Abby and Ella were the apples of Rose and Tom's eye. They were still young enough to really enjoy visiting their grandparents. In the long summer holidays, they sometimes stayed for weeks at a time just loving the beach and all that Bayfield had to offer.

"So, what time should we expect you? I presume you'll be staying for lunch?"

"Well, Abby has figure skating in the afternoon at four thirty, so I reckon if we aim to get to you around ten thirty we could have an early lunch and be on the road back to London by three."

Rose nodded thinking to herself that both Abby and Ella belonged to too many things. There was soccer, swimming, Guides and Brownies, ballet, gymnastics, and now figure skating.

She didn't, however, raise her concerns, but instead said, "Great, we look forward to seeing you all then." Rose was about to put the phone down when Jessica said, "Mom, I heard that there had been a murder somewhere near Ben Miller. Weren't Dad and you going on a retreat somewhere in that neck of the woods?"

Rose went quiet. Her daughter Jessica hated the fact that she had been involved in a number of murder investigations in and around the village of Bayfield.

"Mom, please don't tell me that you were somehow involved with this murder?"

"Now Jessica," Rose said calmly, "I'll tell you about it on Saturday. I must go now. See you then."

No sooner had Rose put the phone down when it rang once again. It was Anne calling from Dartmouth, Nova Scotia.

"Hi, Mom. Did you and Dad enjoy the Couples Retreat?"

Anne and Alan had given them the getaway as a present thinking that it would be relaxing and something a bit different for their parents. It had been a very generous and thoughtful gift.

"Oh, darling, we did enjoy it and yes, it certainly was a different weekend. Thank you so much. Now, how is darling Oliver and baby Gracie?"

Anne had given birth to little Gracie the previous November. Oliver, their two-year-old son had been madly jealous. Tom and Rose had flown out and had spent two weeks primarily pandering to Oliver's every whim.

"Oh, Mom, she's so good and she's actually sleeping through the night already."

"And what about Oliver? How's our little boy?"

"He's much better, mom. I think he actually quite likes his little sister now that Gracie laughs at everything he does."

"What about Alan? Is he working as hard as he was in January?"

Alan was an astrophysicist and a senior professor at Dalhousie University. The last time Rose and Tom had seen their son-in-law he had looked highly stressed out and a prime candidate for a nervous breakdown.

"Mom, would it be okay if we came to visit you in August?"

"Darling, that would be fabulous. We could put the kids in Dad's study and Alan and you can have the guest room."

"But what about Paul, Mom? Isn't he thinking of coming home this summer with Atsuko?"

Paul, their youngest, had met and married a lovely Japanese girl, Atsuko whilst teaching English in Japan. Atsuko was a fashion designer and had started up a line of children's clothing. Gracie and Oliver both sported little outfits designed by their aunt.

Two years previous, Paul had been offered a position at Fanshawe College in London and had returned to Canada. Atsuko had stayed on in Japan, reluctant to leave her thriving business and they had been separated for two years.

Jessica, Paul's sister, had been particularly upset about their split as she had become quite good friends with her Japanese sister-in-law and she had resented her brother for leaving her behind in Japan.

Last summer, Atsuko's father had died quite suddenly, and she had fallen into a deep depression. Paul had flown out and somehow, miraculously, the two had rekindled their love. He had taken a sabbatical from Fanshawe but soon his year would be up and, if he wanted to keep his position, he would have to return.

Rose and Tom had waited with baited breath to see what the outcome would be. Would Atsuko return with him or stay in Japan?

Rose answered Anne with a simple, "I don't know Paul's plans, my love. We'll just have to wait and see. Now, I must go. Thank Alan from both of us for the lovely weekend. Love to all of you."

She put the phone down and continued to prepare their supper. It had been such a long day, they would probably go to bed early. Tom had scheduled a golf game the next day with his friend Doug, and Rose had arranged to meet up with Karen Huber for coffee.

Poor Karen had phoned earlier in a real state of panic. The other couples on the retreat had only been told about the murder at lunch time after they had finished their skits.

Naturally they had looked around and realized that Tom and Rose were missing, and this gave rise to huge speculation.

Rose had calmed her friend down on the phone and had promised to fill her in with all the details the next day.

Rose sighed as she peeled some potatoes and chopped up the carrots. Why was she always such a magnet for murder?

NINE

S usan finished typing up her notes and then checked her emails. Smiling to herself she opened an email from Dr. Ian Green, the forensic pathologist from Goderich. He had sent her his preliminary findings of the death of Juliet Carmichael. His full report could not be filed until the toxicology results had come through from the laboratory and that could take up to a week.

Susan scanned his report quickly, severe bruising to the middle of the back, bruising at the side of the head consistent with a vice like grip, and separation of the skull from the first vertebra, medically known as an atlanto-occipital disarticulation. Death would have been instant.

Susan closed her eyes and tried to visualize the murderer coming up from behind an unsuspecting Juliet, grabbing her head like a vice with both hands and possibly using his foot on her back to act as leverage, then, with a firm twist of the neck, the swift act of murder would have been done.

Susan, still deep in thought, opened up her other emails and found the SOC report. She scanned the list of items found in and around Ivy Cottage looking for any evidence that they could use.

There was nothing out of the ordinary found and so she went back to the medical examiner's report. Had there been any sign of rape? No, but there were signs of sexual activity.

Traces of semen would have to be matched with that of her husband, Harry, although when he had been interviewed he had denied having had sex with his wife that night.

Susan clicked out of the report and put her laptop back into its case. Her stomach was grumbling. She had missed lunch and was now feeling starving.

Leaving the Lion's Hall, Susan walked past the cute bed and breakfast called The Secret Garden, along past the Bayfield Spa and Brandon's Hardware until she got to the Main Street. The Albion beckoned to Susan with the smell of hamburgers and fries wafting through the doors.

Outside the Albion at least twenty bikes, mostly Harley Davidson's, were lined up. Susan entered the building only to find the bar heaving with people. It was so busy that she had to elbow her way up to the bar where, miraculously, tucked into the corner, was an empty bar stool not yet been claimed by anyone.

Sitting on a stool next to Susan was a biker, well at least Susan presumed him to be by the fact that the man wore a worn leather jacket. He sported grey-tinged, long hair tied back in a pony tail and his face was lined and rugged, well seasoned, Susan thought, and rather attractive in a bad-boy kind of way.

She placed her order for a pint of Guinness to which the biker turned and smilingly said, "Are you from Ireland?"

Susan could tell immediately from the gentle lilt in his voice that he himself was indeed from the Fair Isle.

"Oh, no, I'm second generation Canadian and I've never been to Ireland. But I detect that you are connected to the Emerald Isle yourself, am I right?"

"Yes, I've been here in Canada for almost twenty years now, but somehow haven't lost my accent."

"Do you own one of those Harley's out there?" Susan asked, looking in the direction of the front of the building.

"Sure, that's just one of my beauties, I own three. My wife used to say that I loved my bikes more than I cared for her."

"And do you?" Susan said just realizing that he looked the spitting image of Kevin Costner.

The biker went quiet and then said, "By the way, my name is Tony, but you can call me Tone, everyone does."

"Well, my name is Susan and I hate being called Sue. Pleased to meet you, um...Tone."

Susan held out her hand to be shaken. "So, what brings you to Bayfield?"

"Since I retired I joined this bikers group and from May to September we come to Bayfield every Sunday. The owner here has been great in accommodating all of us."

"Where do you bike from?" Susan asked.

"Oh, most of us are from London, although I actually live just outside in Delaware."

"Oh, my sister used to live there. They lived on Thames Street."

"Well, bless my soul, that's where I live. What a co-incidence. What's your sister's name?"

"Mary, but they moved to Calgary over ten years ago."

"My wife had a good friend called Mary."

Once again, he had mentioned his wife, Susan thought. *I wonder if she is still part of his life or have they gone their separate ways?*

"So, you live here in Bayfield?" Tone asked pleasantly.

Susan was about to answer when they were interrupted by the server bringing her lunch. It was a huge hamburger with a mountain of fries. She dug into the meal barely stopping to acknowledge Tone who sat and watched her with a bemused look on his face.

"Boy, you sure were hungry."

Susan wiped her mouth with a serviette and smiled, "Yes, I was starving. Now I feel much better." She looked at her watch. If she wanted to interview Dr. Miller and his wife Sonja before the evening, she would have to get a move on. Susan called the waitress over and asked for her bill. Standing up she put out her hand to Tone and said, "It was so nice chatting to you, Tone."

Tone held out his hand and grasped Susan's, holding it a fraction longer than was necessary for a hand shake. He looked at her and smiled. "I do hope that we will meet again. I should be back here again next Sunday, if not before. Maybe we could have lunch together then?"

Susan thought, why not, but she wasn't sure if she would be free the following week.

"I'll try to make it if work permits."

Tone stood up and watched Susan as she walked out of the Albion. She was certainly one hell of a looker. He wondered what she did for a living working on a Saturday.

TEN

SUNDAY

Karen Huber was waiting for Rose at the Charles Street Market coffee shop. She was an attractive woman of Rose's age but looked much younger with her petite figure and elfin good looks. Karen's husband Brian was also quite youthful in appearance.

"Hi, Karen, "Rose said as she walked in, "Have you got your coffee?"

"Oh, yes, I arrived here a little early."

"Do you want a muffin? I'm having one. The Morning Glory are to die for." Rose said and when Karen declined she had a revelation. That was why Karen was so slim and she was so plump!

"So, Rose, what happened to you and Tom? One minute you were in the room and the next you had both disappeared? When they announced that a dead body had been found I immediately thought that it was you, Rose. You had me quite frightened."

"Well, it's a long story..." Rose relayed everything that had happened concluding with the police arriving and

Harry's devastation after they found his wife's body in the cabin.

"I knew that Harry and Juliet were having marital problems because I overheard them arguing, but I'm not sure if he murdered his wife or not? The man I saw Juliet talking to outside didn't look like Harry, although I really could only see the outline of the person. He didn't look as heavy set as Harry. In fact, the more I think about it, whoever it was, looked definitely quite slight."

Karen looked thoughtful. "They do say that ninety percent of couple's murders are instigated by one or another of the partners. In France they call it crime de passion, a crime of passion. But if Harry didn't murder his wife, then who on earth did?'

"That dear Karen, I intend to find out."

"Oh, Rose, you're not going to do your sleuthing again, are you?"

"Not really, Karen, but I am intrigued by it all. I can't help having an enquiring mind."

"Just be careful. Promise me you won't go charging in like you did last year."

Karen was referring to the previous year when Rose had tackled the doctor and had been severely kicked in her head. She was very lucky to be alive.

"Changing the subject somewhat, Rose, Brian is in the finals of a knockout curling championship tomorrow at the Maitland in Goderich. I've got a couple of spare tickets and wondered if Tom and you would like to come?"

"Wow, I never knew that Brian was a curler. Yes, we would love to come along. What time?"

The two women chatted away amicably for another half an hour and then they both got up to leave. Karen touched

Rose's shoulder and said, "What did you honestly think of the couples retreat, Rose?"

"Well, Karen, I know that Tom was very reluctant to participate in what he called new-age nonsense, but I think that he actually enjoyed some of the exercises, particularly the introduction when we had to look into each other's eyes. He was quite cut up because he felt that Juliet had been trying to reach out to him through her eyes. She obviously made a big impact on him. If she wasn't dead, I'd probably be madly jealous by now."

Karen laughed, "Brian felt the same way as Tom, but I don't think that he enjoyed any one of the exercises. Poor man, I pretty well had to drag him along. There were some couples who seemed rather intense. Dr. Seb Miller and Sonja, what were they, sex therapists? Well, they didn't seem very happy as a couple, if you ask me."

Rose looked interested. "Why, what do you mean, Karen? What gave you the impression that they were unhappy?"

"Oh, just their body language and I overheard Sonja snap at Seb during our skits."

They had reached Karen's car and Rose turned to give Karen a big hug before saying goodbye. They would be at the curling rink the next day to cheer Brian and his team along.

Rose walked back home in deep thought. Something Karen had said was niggling at the back of her mind. Oh, it would come to her eventually, she thought.

After returning home, Rose busied herself with getting lunch for Tom, putting together a sweet potato, onion, and garlic frittata and a crisp, Greek salad. Tom was out playing golf, but he had promised to be back by one p.m.

True to his word, bang on one o'clock, Tom came through

the front door accompanied by a loud cacophony of barking from the dogs.

"How did your coffee morning go, love?" Tom asked Rose as he sat up at the kitchen table waiting for his lunch to be served.

"Oh, it was good. I really do like Karen. She's invited us to the Curling Championship tomorrow in Goderich. Do you even know where the curling club is Tom?"

Tom shook his head. He didn't really have much to do with Goderich, although he had played a few games of golf at The Sunset Acres Golf Course just north of Goderich. He wasn't even aware that there was a curling club in Goderich.

"I never knew that Brian curled."

"Well, he must be quite good if he's in the Championships," Rose said while serving up a plate of the frittata and salad.

Tom had been checking his iPhone while Rose had been talking. "Ah, ha, I've found the curling club. Well, I never knew that. It's part of the Maitland Valley Golf Course, next to the clubhouse. What time did you say we had to be there, love?"

"Karen said that they would pick us up around 6:30 in the evening, why, have you got something on tomorrow?"

Tom was thoughtful. "Yes, but I'll be back by late afternoon. I'm taking Doug over in the afternoon to the London Science and Health Centre. He has to have an MRI."

Rose looked alarmed. Doug and Irene had been their friends ever since they had first moved to the village. Doug and Tom were regular golfing buddies and Irene and Rose often met for coffee. "Why does he need an MRI?"

Tom looked uncomfortable. "You see, the thing is, love, I really shouldn't have mentioned it at all. Doug asked me to keep it to myself, so I haven't said anything to anyone. He's been having trouble breathing. They thought that it was asthma but now he's been coughing up blood. It doesn't look good, love."

"Oh, dear," Rose whispered, "I do hope that it's not anything too awful."

They had lost far too many friends in the village over the past few years. Somehow losing so many people had been a big reckoning for Tom and Rose. It was funny how when you were younger death was so far removed from one's awareness and then suddenly the finality of life slowly seemed to creep up on you, Rose thought. Poor Doug and Irene.

The telephone rang making both Tom and Rose jump. With a heavy heart Rose answered, "Rose Blair speaking."

"Hi, Mom, it's Paul."

Rose silently mouthed to Tom, "It's Paul."

"Hi, darling," she said, and they proceeded to chat for the following half hour. Finally, Rose handed the phone over to Tom to speak to their son.

The upshot of their conversation was that Paul and Atsuko were coming back to Canada in June. Paul would be resuming his position at Fanshawe College, but the most exciting news of all was that Atsuko was expecting a baby. This time she was happy to be leaving Japan to be with Paul in London.

"Oh Tom, that's the best news I've heard in ages. Just think, another little grandchild."

They already had four grandchildren, three granddaughters, Abby, Ella, and baby Gracie and, so far, just one darling little grandson, Oliver.

Tom smiled brightly and suddenly, for once, the world seemed a better place.

ELEVEN

S usan pulled up outside a split ranch style house on Warren Street, Goderich. She had phoned ahead of time just to make sure that the Millers were going to be at home. Before setting out Susan had done a quick Google search on sex therapy.

She had been quite mind boggled by the statistics on the scale of male impotency and how the use of sex therapy as a response to dealing with the problem had grown accordingly. Often the impotency was connected to depression and sometimes to do with the medication prescribed for depression. It appeared to be a vicious circle whichever way you looked at it.

Susan knocked on the door and it was opened by an attractive middle-aged woman, Sonja she presumed. However, on entering the living room, there was seated another attractive woman, a bit younger than the first. She stood up and introduced herself as Sonja.

"Seb is in the study. I'll just go and get him, unless Deb, you wouldn't mind?"

Deb returned with Seb Miller in tow.

"Good evening, it's Detective Parker, isn't it?"

"My full title is Detective Chief Inspector Parker, but you can call me Susan."

They shook hands and then Seb introduced the two women in the house.

"This is Sonja, and this is Deb. Just to be clear we are not actually married, in fact, we are all in a polyamorous relationship."

Susan's eyebrows must have shot up because Seb hastily added, "Oh, it's perfectly legal as long as we're not married. I suppose you're here to ask me about the dreadful murder at the couple's retreat?"

Susan had never come across anyone so self assured as the good doctor and she had never met anyone who was in a ménage a-trois. She did think that it was somewhat ironic that Seb Miller was a sex therapist.

"Umm...is your partner Sonja, also a qualified sex therapist?"

"Why of course, yes and Deb is too. That's where we all met, at school."

"Right, well, did you know the deceased, Juliet Carmichael?"

Susan had pulled out her iPad and had started to type. This was the first year that she had not handwritten her witness statements and it felt decidedly awkward using her electronics, but head office had insisted that they go paperless come what may.

Seb Miller started to talk and Susan noticed he had lost some of his blustering.

"Yes, I had met Juliet Carmichael several times before the retreat. She is...um I mean, was a nurse at the Goderich hospital. I broke my wrist a few months ago and she was the nurse in charge at the emergency room.

"Did you ever socialize with her outside of the hospital?"

Seb went very still and then said, "Could we please conduct this interview in the privacy of my study?"

It was painfully obvious that he didn't want either Sonja or Deb to overhear what he had to say.

"Yes, certainly, lead the way," Susan said and followed Seb into his study.

There were several certificates showing his various qualifications from three different universities, hanging on the wall, plus there were some photographs of both Sonja and Deb. Susan noticed that in one picture, looking very glamorous and in full evening garb, Seb and Sonja were standing next to someone who looked remarkably like Stephen Harper and his wife, probably at some fundraising event or other.

"Okay, doctor, spill the beans. Tell me about your relationship with Juliet Carmichael because I presume that's what you didn't want the other two women in your life to hear?"

Seb looked for once somewhat abashed and coughed before answering. "She was an attractive woman. We bumped into each other after that first meeting at the hospital at the Y in Goderich and then one thing led to another."

Susan waited for him to elaborate. She had learnt that by keeping quiet invariably the person being interviewed would eventually talk unprompted.

"We had incredible sex together. I can tell you for certain that she didn't have a good relationship with her husband. In fact, he was a control freak, I mean, big time."

"So, I gather that Sonja and Deb didn't know about your affair? As you already have a polygamous relationship, why would they mind if you had multiple affairs?"

Seb was quiet for a while before answering. "There is a

difference between having an open relationship and an affair you know. I was perfectly aware that Juliet would never leave Harry. It was just a fling thing and anyway we split up a few months ago after only a few weeks of intense passion. I got the impression that Juliet had moved on to another love interest."

"Why would Harry and Juliet even contemplate going on a couple's retreat, particularly one that was facilitated by you?"

"Deep down, Juliet really loved Harry and she so wanted their marriage to work. I had often told her that they both needed counselling and I suppose she saw the couple's retreat as just that."

"Okay, Seb, where were you around two in the morning? I have to ask."

Dr. Seb Miller laughed and once again pumped up his self-assurance, "Well, I was in bed with Sonja, but I doubt if she would be able to verify that as she herself was sound asleep. No, DCI Parker, I did not murder Juliet. Honestly, why would I? We had already gone our separate ways."

Susan was inclined to believe him even though his bombastic attitude irritated her.

"I will have to interview both Sonja and Deb. Could you send Sonja in please on your way out?" Susan said crisply, all business now.

Sonja entered the study. Her blonde hair was tied back in a single ropey braid. She was wearing a brightly patterned yellow and red caftan and Susan thought that she looked somewhat like an aging hippy.

"So, Sonja, was this the first time that you had met Juliet Carmichael at the retreat?"

"Yes, but I had heard about her. My brother James has not stopped talking about her since he was introduced about six weeks ago."

"James?" Susan said remembering the argument that Rose had overheard in the farmhouse kitchen.

"Yes, they had started a bit of a relationship. I warned my brother not to get involved, I mean, from what I had heard, Juliet was nothing more than a maneater."

Susan must have looked shocked because Sonja added quickly, "Yes, I knew about Seb and her, but I also knew that it wouldn't last, which it didn't."

"If you knew about your partner's affair surely you couldn't have been very happy?"

Sonja looked surprised. "DCI Parker, when your partner has an insatiable hunger for sex like Seb you actually are more than happy to let someone else satisfy that desire. No, I bore no grudge against Juliet and before you even ask, I certainly did not kill her."

"Right," she was nothing but frank, Susan thought, "Okay, I'm finished with you for now, Sonja, could you ask Deb to step in on your way out. Thanks, oh, and before you go, I will need to get your brother James' contact information."

Deb was a good ten years younger than Sonja. She was petite and dark haired with large, liquid brown eyes and a perfect rosebud mouth.

"Okay, Deb, this won't take long. I know that you were not present at the couples retreat, but I do want to ask you if you actually knew Juliet Carmichael?"

Deb shook her pretty head, "I did know of her, but I'd never actually met her in person. Sonja and I often talked about the other love interests in Seb's life. I'm afraid we were not very kind. I mean, I'm sure that Sonja has told you about Seb and his affairs?"

"Umm.... Yes, I mean Sonja told me, but Seb is under the

impression that you both were unaware of his relationship with Juliet."

Deb laughed, "Yes, that's pure Seb, sneaking around. There's not much that gets past Sonja and I, I can tell you that for sure.

"What about Harry, Juliet's husband? Did you ever meet him?"

"James, Sonja's brother, is on the same curling team as Harry, so she's heard quite a bit about him through James. According to James, Harry is one manipulative jerk of a husband."

Susan smiled as Deb's description of Harry could have been that of her own ex, the jerk, with the only difference being that Harry and Juliet had been married for fifteen years and Susan and her ex had only been together for five years. *How could she have stayed with such a pig of a husband for so long,* Susan thought.

"So, what about James and Juliet? Were they having a serious affair?"

"No, I very much doubt it. Juliet had a history of brief affairs so likely James would have probably been ditched sooner rather than later."

Susan looked at her watch. It was almost eight o'clock and she was exhausted. It was time to call it quits. Taking her leave of the ménage a trois, Susan drove back to Bayfield full of thoughts of polygamy. In all cases that she had, ever heard of, it always was the man who had the multiple wives. Had there ever been cases of women having multiple husbands?

On arriving back to her Harbour Court condo, Susan poured herself out a stiff drink, stripped off her clothing, leaving them in a pile on the carpeted floor, and ran naked out into her hot tub which was located against her courtyard wall.

This too had been a recent acquisition, along with the Porsche. The hot tub had formed an integral part of Susan's regime of me time and she loved both her new toys passionately.

TWELVE

MONDAY

After her relaxing soak in the hot tub, Susan had slept like a baby and had woken up feeling thoroughly refreshed and ready for her morning run. Putting on her running shoes she left her condo and ran down Jowett's Road to the marina where she turned right and continued to run past the Cottage Colony, past the Boat Chandlery, and around the marina until she reached the beach.

Here Susan ran along the sand and then turned back inland and up the steep hill to Jowett's Road, ending back at her condo. After a quick shower and a cup of coffee she was ready to drive out to Ivy Cottage to interview the rather elusive caretaker, Lydia.

Lydia, it appeared, looked after all the administration for the couple's retreat weekends, handling the registration and finance plus generally managing the smooth running of the farmhouse.

When Susan arrived at Ivy Cottage Lydia was nowhere to be found. Susan finally tracked her down at the back of the property where she was feeding chickens. Susan noticed that

Lydia was dressed all in black and formed quite an austere impression with her severe clothing and short-cropped black hair, almost masculine looking Susan mused as she put out her hand to greet her.

"This won't take long. I just have a few questions to ask you about the couple's weekend."

Lydia nodded and walked back towards the farmhouse where, on entering the kitchen, she put the kettle on and turned to Susan saying abruptly, "Tea or coffee?"

She has no social skills, Susan thought as she answered, "I'd love a cup of tea, please."

"Right," Susan said, all business as she got out her iPad and typed in Lydia's name. "How long have you worked at Ivy Cottage?"

"I've worked here for five years, but only for Seb Miller for two. I get paid extra for each retreat and I can tell you that I earn every penny."

"What does your work actually entail?"

"For the retreats I have to organize the catering and refreshments, make sure all the bedrooms are cleaned with fresh sheets, soaps, shampoos, etc. I also have to prepare the receipts and registration forms, and work with Dr. Miller to have an agenda typed up and printed for each couple. I'm really just a glorified secretary and cleaner rolled into one." Lydia said with a sour look on her face.

"Right, now, had you met the deceased before the weekend?"

Susan liked to go off on a tangent as it helped to throw the witness off balance a bit.

"Um... well, yes and no. You see, I walked in on a rather um... awkward situation late on Saturday night. Everyone had gone to bed really early and I was clearing up and prepping the breakfast table, generally getting ready for the next day, when I heard noises coming from the sunroom," here Lydia paused.

Susan said, "Go on then."

"Well, I walked into the living room, the lights had been turned off, but a couple of candles had been lit in the sunroom. Juliet was lying stark naked on one of the large floor cushions and a man, I'm not at all sure who he was, because all I could see was his naked body on top of Juliet and they were at it like rutting animals."

"What time was this, do you know?"

"Well, it had to have been around midnight although I cannot be sure."

"Had you met Harry Carmichael, Juliet's husband?"

"Yes, I met him when they both checked in on Saturday afternoon. He seemed a moody sort."

"Was the man with Juliet in the sunroom her husband?"

Lydia shook her head emphatically. "No, the man with Juliet was definitely slighter in build, younger I would say and had longish hair. Although I cannot be one hundred percent sure as I only saw a naked back and behind, and even that was in shadow."

"I have to ask you a question. Where were you at two a.m. Sunday morning?"

Lydia laughed, "Well, that's easy, I was tucked up in bed sound asleep, but I have no one to vouch for me."

"Right, well, if you think of anything else here is my card."

Lydia took the card and picked up her tea cup. She hesitated before turning around to say, "There is something else. When Juliet called to pay for the couple's retreat, oh, at least two weeks ago now, her Visa card was rejected with insufficient funds. She brought in cash the next day, but I know that she was really embarrassed."

"Okay, thank you Lydia, you've been most helpful." Susan left Ivy Cottage feeling unsettled. Why did the enigmatic Lydia volunteer so much information? In her long experience of interviewing people, Susan found that normally you had to squeeze the information out of people. What had she learnt though? That Juliet was a woman with loose morals, that went undisputed, but to be having sex downstairs in the sunroom with a stranger while her husband Harry was asleep upstairs in his bedroom, seemed risky to say the least.

Was Lydia to be believed, Susan thought, as she felt the hairs on the back of her neck rise. There was something strange and cold about the woman that she couldn't quite put her finger on.

THIRTEEN

Susan arrived at The Lion's Hall just as the rest of her team were beginning to trickle in. Constable Ryan stood to one side to allow Susan to go by and the rest of the team stood to acknowledge her until she greeted them.

"Good afternoon. Please everyone, take a seat. I'll start the ball rolling with my report."

Susan opened her laptop and quickly glanced at all the messages left for her. She saw the SOC report and another note from Ian Green, the forensics man from Goderich.

"It appears that I also have reports just in from the Scene of Crimes people and also from our forensics guy. So, shall I begin?

"I interviewed Dr. Sebastian Miller and his partner, Sonja and found an interesting twist. They are part of a polygamous relationship. The other partner is Deborah Nock. The two women appeared well aware of Dr. Miller's philandering ways. It appears that he had an affair with the deceased Juliet but had finished the relationship several months ago.

Sonja's brother, James, it so transpires, was the latest love interest and I've yet to interview him. The good doctor is a cheating philanderer, but I do tend to rule him out of the equation as he had no real motive for murder and the same applies to his partners.

"However, I interviewed Lydia Thompson, the administrator and general caretaker of Ivy Cottage and she claims to have witnessed Juliet, and an unknown man, making out in the sunroom late on Saturday night after everyone else had gone to bed.

"The other interesting piece of information that came to light, was that Lydia mentioned that Juliet's credit card was rejected when she went to book and pay for the retreat. How that might be at all relevant to the case, I don't know, but the IT guys are checking out her bank accounts as we speak."

Constable Ryan put up her hand. "Ma'am, has Juliet's phone been found yet?"

"Not as far as I know but let me read the SOC reports."

Susan clicked on the email and scanned the factual report. No phone was mentioned; however, tire tracks and foot prints had been recovered by the side of the road leading to the driveway. Susan relayed all of this to her team.

"If we could find her phone, then I'm sure that we would be able to track from her calls whoever it was that she met up with, and the possibly that this may lead us to her murderer." Susan said looking around the room at her team.

Constable Ryan once more put up her hand.

"Yes, Constable," Susan said.

"I suspect, ma'am that the murderer has the phone, but my question is, does the husband, I mean, Harry, share the same telephone provider and account because if they have a joint plan, then we would be able to trace her calls through Harry's account."

"Good thinking, Constable. Now, let me see, who interviewed the husband?"

Susan scrolled through her notes. Sergeant Flowers put his hand up.

"Ma'am, I interviewed Harry Carmichael."

"Okay, let's be having your report then, Sergeant."

"First of all, I have to say that the husband appeared to be all over the place. One minute he was acting devastated and the next he was one angry man. He acknowledged the fact that his wife had been unfaithful, but, according to him, that was all locked firmly behind them and the couple's retreat was supposed to be part of the healing process. I did ask if he knew where his wife's phone had got to, and he appeared genuinely perplexed as to why she didn't have it on her. She apparently was normally glued to her phone. I never asked about his phone or phone account, but I can make further enquiries on that front. Much as I don't like the man, I really don't think that he is our murderer."

"Thank you, Sergeant. Constable Ryan, you talked to Juliet's work mates at the hospital. What did they have to say about their co-worker?"

Constable Ryan stood up and cleared her throat. She was still nervous about presentations and felt her stomach lurch as she trolled through her notes ready to talk to her team.

"Juliet had three good friends at the hospital, Sara, Brianne, and Nina. They were all genuinely cut up about her death. When asked about her relationship with her husband, all three women pulled faces and berated Harry quite vocally. They couldn't understand why she had stayed with him for so long. He was abusive both mentally and physically. Her friends knew that Juliet was having various affairs and they thought that was fine as she deserved some happiness.

"They didn't mention any specific names, but one of the women, umm... Sara, said that Juliet had appeared nervous and jumpy the last time she had worked with her. When she had asked if she had a problem, Juliet had denied anything was wrong. Sara was convinced that something or someone was causing her friend's nervousness. The rest of the hospital staff all liked Juliet and were shocked by the news of her death. That's all, ma'am."

"Thank you, Constable," Susan said and looked down at her notes. "Constables Brown and Elliot, what did the couples attending the retreat have to say?"

"Right, ma'am. There were six couples on the retreat including Dr. Miller and his wife. The Blair's, Carmichael's, Huber's, Philpot's, and the Wilson's. We've already had reports on the first three couples which brings us to the Huber's, Philpott's, and the Wilson's.

"Karen and Brian Huber live in Waterloo but have a cottage just south of Bayfield. When interviewed they said that they had known Harry Carmichael and Juliet through the curling club. Harry and Brian play on the same team. Karen remarked that she didn't think that the Carmichaels had a particularly happy marriage and she suspected that Harry was an abusive husband.

"The Philpot's are from Kincardine. Jerry Philpott works at Bruce Power and Sheila is a retired teacher. Both said that Juliet had been acting strangely throughout the Saturday evening activities. She had appeared jittery and nervous and Harry behaved moody and sullen.

"Now the Wilsons, umm... Mike and Sandy, noticed Juliet

making several phone calls. They also said that she appeared on edge. That's all I have, ma'am."

"Thank you, Constables, right, well, I have the toxicology results back from the lab and it makes for interesting reading. It appears that Juliet Carmichael had a significant quantity of cocaine in her bloodstream and traces of cocaine in her nostrils. She must have snorted a considerable amount of cocaine for there still to be residual traces in her nasal passages. We need to find out if Juliet had a serious addiction problem or was her use of cocaine purely recreational? Sergeant Flowers, I would like you to re-interview the husband and ask him about Juliet's habit. Don't pussy foot around, we need to know if her use of drugs has any bearing on this murder."

"Okay, everyone, it appears that our victim was well liked by everyone although there seems to be no love lost between her husband and herself. Somewhere around twelve and two in the morning, Juliet met up with someone and was observed walking down the lane with them, was seen having sex with a person other than her husband and was then murdered.

"Who is this mystery person or persons? So far team, we have very little to go on, no motive for murder. In fact, we have diddly squat, just a few hints that Harry her husband was abusive and that Juliet herself was a bit of a player, none of which gives us a strong enough motive for murder. We need to dig deeper.

"Now that we know Juliet used drugs I want you to go back and re-interview everyone. Someone will, I'm sure, be privy to her drug use. Constable Ryan, I would like you to make a list of all known drug suppliers in this area. Juliet must have got the cocaine from someone. Find the supplier and then we might be a bit closer to finding out more about our victim.

Right, go to it everyone and bring back something that we can work with."

The team dispersed, and Susan sat a while longer deep in thought. They really had very little to go on. The case was beginning to go cold on them even before it had really got started and that worried Susan.

FOURTEEN

aren and Brian Huber called for Tom and Rose promptly at six thirty. They chatted amicably for the twenty-minute journey to Goderich and Rose was once more struck with the thought that Karen was such a lovely, warm, and friendly person.

They arrived at the Maitland Golf and Curling Club and Brian went off to join his fellow curling team whilst Karen, Rose, and Tom made their way to the bar. Shortly afterwards the teams appeared on the ice which was separated from the bar area by a glass wall.

Rose immediately recognized Harry Carmichael, although he somehow looked different, more commanding then before. He certainly did not look like the grieving widow. There appeared much laughing and back slapping as the curling teams were introduced to each other.

Rose turned to Karen and said, "Why do they all seem so pleased with themselves, Karen?"

Karen laughed, "Well, they did win the championship cup

last week at St. Thomas. Actually, it was Harry Carmichael who took the winning rock."

"He doesn't seem to be missing his wife," Rose said and then bit her lip afterwards. It was a rather tactless remark, but Karen just laughed again and said, "Oh, Rose, that's why I like you so much. You just say what other people are thinking. It's really quite refreshing.

"But you're quite right, Harry doesn't appear to be particularly broken hearted by his wife's death. Oh, look over there, Rose, that's James who has just come in. He's the one Juliet was flirting outrageously with a few weeks ago. If you ask me, I would say that they were having an affair."

Rose looked closely at James. He was a slight man, in his late forties, handsome in a clean, fresh boyish way. He reminded Rose of Robert Kennedy, not traditionally handsome but he had something about him that turned the eye. He appeared very down in spirits and barely looked up when the team started their warm up. Rose watched him as he wandered over to the bar, ordered a beer, and then sauntered over to the window where he appeared to be watching Harry. Rose hoped that there would not be any confrontational scene or fight. She waited and held her breath as Harry looked up at James. For one minute his face clouded over and Rose was convinced that he was going to come up and confront James. Then he shook his head and turned his back on his wife's lover and the game began in earnest.

Rose made up her mind. She walked over to James and, putting her hand on his shoulder, she quietly said, "I'm so sorry for what happened to Juliet Carmichael."

He spun around so fast that Rose was almost knocked over. From closeup she could see that his face was tormented and ravaged with grief. He began to splutter and deny knowing

Juliet well and then he said, "I can't keep up this pretence anymore. I loved Juliet with my whole heart and soul and that pig of a husband over there never deserved her."

His eyes welled up as Rose led him to a chair and urged him to sit down. "I am really sorry, James. I met Juliet last weekend at the retreat and she was a special and beautiful woman, of that I am sure. Had you known her long?"

James sniffed and produced a hankie from his pocket. Blowing his nose loudly he looked at Rose with his deep, sad eyes.

"Well, we had been umm... been seeing each other for a few weeks now. In fact, I told her about the couple's retreat at Ben Miller as my sister Sonja works with her husband as a facilitator at the retreat. I wish that I had never mentioned it to her. It's all my fault."

His voice began to waver, and Rose could see how deeply upset he was. "If I hadn't had gone out to Ivy Cottage and arranged to meet Juliet, then that bastard of a husband would never have killed the only person in the world whom I have ever loved."

Interesting, Rose thought, James obviously believed that Harry had murdered Juliet. So, it appeared that James was the man she had seen with Juliet outside in the middle of the night? She looked at him again and tried to recall the image she had seen of the two of them walking down the driveway of Ivy Cottage. It was dark between the trees and the two figures were back lit by the rising moon. *I suppose it could have been him*, Rose thought, *but I wouldn't want to swear on a bible that it was.*

She looked over to where Tom was engaged in a conversation with Harry. She hoped that James didn't do anything rash as he was an emotional wreck and could obviously be unpredictable in his behaviour.

The curling began, and Karen, Tom, and Rose cheered on Brian's team. Harry was clearly the star of the team and appeared to be in his element.

Rose couldn't help thinking about the conversation that she had overheard in the kitchen at Ivy Cottage between Harry and Juliet. He had obviously known about her friendship with James, but Juliet had denied that they were having any sort of relationship although she had said that he was a married man.

Rose looked around to where James was still intently watching the curling team. There did not appear to be a woman with him. Rose got up and ambled back over to him. "Are you alright? Did you come by yourself? You can join us if you want, we're over there." Rose pointed to where Karen and Tom were sitting.

"Umm... well I did come by myself, but I'm not good company right now. But thank you all the same." And for the first time that evening he smiled and immediately Rose could see the attraction of the man. His smile lit his face up like a beacon. "You have been most kind listening to me. I truly appreciate it. Thank you." With that James turned and walked out of the building. It was eight o'clock.

Rose went back over to Karen and Tom.

"So, you were over talking to James, I see. You know that he used to be on the curling team and that's where Juliet would have first met him." Karen said.

"Isn't he married?" Rose said remembering Juliet and Harry's conversation.

"Well, I think that he's been separated from his wife for oh, maybe a year. He was one of the team's best curlers and then he appeared to just lose all interest. Everyone put it down to his marriage split."

There was a loud triumphant shout as Harry put his rock dead centre and the game was declared over, with the Goderich team the victors. The Maitland Curlers had won again, and Harry Carmichael's look of triumph fairly radiated the room. Soon afterwards, Brian joined them for some celebratory drinks and then it was time to go home. They drove back to Bayfield with Rose deep in thought.

FIFTEEN

While Rose, Tom, Karen, and Brian had been at the curling club, DCI Susan Parker had been curled up on the sofa in her red satin PJ's re-reading all the reports pertaining to the investigation of the murder of Juliet Carmichael.

She felt extremely frustrated as there appeared to be absolutely no leads with very little to go on other than the toxicology reports which showed high levels of cocaine in Juliet's blood stream.

Susan knew that there were many people who took drugs mostly for recreational use and they were not murdered. However, cocaine was notoriously expensive and if Juliet had an addiction then the cost of sustaining her habit would probably put a drain on her bank account, hence the rejected credit card, Susan thought.

Of course, this was simply speculation and there could be a very simple explanation for the rejected credit card which was totally unconnected to the case. They would have to wait until the IT guys from London got back to them with their report on Juliet's bank account. *Far too many lose ends still,* Susan thought as she got off the sofa and began to pace the room.

It was then that she thought about James, Sonja's brother and supposed lover of the deceased. Nobody had yet interviewed him. Susan looked at the clock on the living room wall. It was just eight-thirty, still early enough to catch someone in. She picked up her phone and tapped in James' number.

The phone rang for ages before finally being answered by someone who sounded out of breath, he had clearly run to pick up the phone.

"James speaking."

"Oh, hi, James. My name is DCI Susan Parker and I would like to talk to you about your relationship with Juliet Carmichael. Are you around tomorrow morning?"

There was a pause on the other end of the line before James finally answered, "Actually no, tomorrow I have clients booked all day."

"Oh, I see," Susan said, "well, what about this evening? I see by your 524 number that you live in Goderich. I could be at your place within say twenty minutes."

Another long pause before James let out a deep sigh and said, "I might as well get it over and done with. I live on East Street. I'll be waiting for you."

Susan put her phone down and dashed to her bedroom where she threw off her PJ's and quickly dressed in a casual sweater and jeans. She grabbed her iPad and purse on her way out and jumped into her Porsche. She arrived outside James house fifteen minutes later and knocked on the door.

The door was opened by a tousled haired man who looked to be in his early forties. His eyes looked puffy and red and his cheeks were all blotchy. There was something so profoundly sad about the man that Susan wanted to put her arms around and embrace him. Instead she showed him her warrant card and suggested that they go into the living room to talk.

"Okay, it is James Anderson, isn't it?" Susan said as she typed his name into her iPad. "What do you do for a living?"

"I'm a chiropractor."

"Is your practise here in Goderich?"

"Oh, yes, on the Square. I've had my practise there for the past five years."

"Oh, right, well James, you probably know why I'm here so let's just cut to the chase. We know from our enquiries that you and the deceased, Juliet Carmichael, were having an affair. I want to ask you a few questions about your relationship with her?"

"Have you not arrested the murderer?" James suddenly shouted, and Susan backed away. His whole demeanour looked like a volcano just waiting to explode.

"Who do you mean, James?" Susan asked quietly.

"That pig of a husband, of course, who else do you think? It's pretty obvious that he killed her so what I don't understand is why you have to harass people like me when you should be arresting the husband."

His voice broke as he gulped back a sob.

"We don't know yet who killed her, but for now we have to leave no stone unturned. Humour me. Tell me all about your relationship with Juliet Carmichael."

James went very quiet and then started to talk in a monotone voice. "She was like a breath of fresh air, always excited about everything. She loved life and living and I'm pretty certain that she loved me."

"What about her husband? Did she love Harry?" Susan

asked quietly not wishing to stir the volcano inside James again.

"I will never understand to this day why she stayed with him all these years. He was physically and mentally abusive to her all the time. Just because they had been high school sweet hearts she felt that she owed him her loyalty."

"Well, it didn't stop her from sleeping around though, did it, James. I believe that she was quite free with her favours?"

James had turned quite pale.

"What do you mean free with her favours?"

"She was seeing other men before she met you. But what I really wanted to know is did you know anything about her drug problem?"

Once again James went extremely still. Susan was about to continue when he quietly said, "She never actually told me, but I knew. Her eyes were permanently darting about the place and her pupils always seemed to be hugely dilated.

Her energy level surpassed anyone I knew. Oh, and she had frequent nose bleeds too. I have a medical background, so I know the signs, but I never confronted her. I know several doctors and nurses who I suspect use drugs to keep themselves going. It's not uncommon."

"Do you know who her supplier was, then?"

"I don't know who her direct supplier was, but it is commonly known around here that if you want to purchase drugs go and speak to certain families in the Mennonite community. With family connections in Mexico the trafficking of drugs into this area is relatively easy."

Susan knew something about the Mennonite connection. The London Drug Squad was onto it but hadn't yet succeeded in making any inroads into finding the mules importing the drugs into this area.

"What about Juliet's financial situation? Cocaine doesn't come cheap."

"Oh, I knew nothing about her finances. You should be talking to her husband, he is the accountant and I'm sure that he controlled everything that Juliet spent, just as he took control of her life."

"So, you have no idea where she got her drugs from other than, possibly, from a contact in the Mennonite community?"

"I'm afraid I can't help you there. Now if you don't mind I need you to leave now. I feel emotionally drained and it's been a long evening. I was at the curling championships before you arrived, and you should have seen that rat Harry Carmichael. He was not exactly grieving. If you are looking for a suspect then he's your man, believe me."

Susan departed feeling unsettled. James, she felt had over-played the mourning lover. Was he as clueless as he made out? She drove back to Bayfield along Highway 21 oblivious to the fact that she was doing well over speed limit.

SIXTEEN

TUESDAY

Rose and Tom woke to pouring rain. Ben and Puff took one look at the downpour and refused to go outside when Tom got up to let them out. He had gone straight back to bed followed by the two dogs.

Rose stretched her arms up in the air and jumped out of bed.

"Why don't you stay and cuddle up to me a bit longer, love. It's a foul day outside. Have you anything planned for today?"

Rose thought about it for a while and then softly tip toed over to the side table where she had left her planner and phone. These days she relied rather heavily on her planner and tried to make a point of looking at it first thing in the morning. She glanced at her watch. It was eight thirty. If she rushed she could go to the fitness class, but on the other hand, she could just go back to bed and cuddle up to Tom like he had suggested. She had no meetings or appointments to keep, in fact, unusually for Rose, her day was completely clear. If it wasn't for the inclement weather, she might even have suggested to Tom that they go for a little road trip, maybe to the village of Elora which Rose had ear marked as place that she wanted to visit. Choosing going back to bed over fitness class, Rose snuggled up to Tom.

"Are you feeling a bit better today, Tom?"

"Yes love. I slept well, and I'm no longer haunted by the memory of Juliet's eyes. Do you fancy going out for lunch today, maybe going to Goderich for a change?"

Rose smiled. Tom's idea of a lunch date was going to the A&W which she didn't mind as the hamburgers were really quite good, but she did fancy something a little more up market and different.

"Well, yes, but should we try maybe the Park Tower restaurant. I've never been there before, and I believe that it's quite good."

"Sure, do you think we need to make reservations?"

"No, I doubt it this time of the year. Okay, that's settled then. We'll do some shopping first while we're in Goderich and then have lunch. Great!"

Rose picked up her book. It was the latest Peter Robinson and she was so enjoying it. Tom gently took the book away from her and pulled Rose to him.

"I thought that we might explore our inner souls," he said with a twinkle in his eyes.

Rose laughed and threw her arms around him. They were interrupted by the telephone ringing. "Leave it alone, love." Tom said huskily, but Rose had already jumped out of bed to reach for the phone.

It was her sister Kate calling from Kelowna. Rose looked at her bedside clock. She was quite shocked to see that it was already nine which meant that it was only six o'clock in the morning in B.C. Why on earth would her sister be phoning so early in the day?

"Oh, Rose," Kate barked down the phone. She had a very loud, distinctive voice.

Tom could hear her every word from the other side of the room. "What's wrong, Kate?"

"Well, I've just been served with divorce papers. I couldn't sleep a wink last night. That rotten pig of a husband wants half of everything now. We've already sold the farm and I thought that was it when I bought this condo and now it looks as if I'll have to sell this as well. What am I to do?"

After Bob had gone off with Kate's best friend, Natalie, he had said that Kate could keep their small hobby farm, but she had decided that it was all too much work feeding the livestock and keeping the maintenance of the five-acre property.

Rose and Tom had encouraged Kate to buy a small condo and they were thrilled when she had taken their advice and found a lovely place overlooking the lake. *Just what was Bob playing at now*, Rose thought.

"Calm down, Kate. Have you spoken to your lawyers yet?"

"I'm almost too scared to. Every time I have a conversation with them I'm billed another couple of hundred dollars."

"So, what's brought this on? I thought that everything had been settled?"

"Well, so did I, but apparently Natalie and Bob have found a small winery they want to buy, and they need more capital. Bob says that by law he should get half of everything."

"What a stinking rat." Rose exclaimed while her heart felt so heavy for her poor sister.

"You know, Kate, have you thought about moving back here? Property is so much cheaper here, and you would be able to buy a lovely house for the price of your condo."

"Well, actually, I had thought of that which is why I'm calling. Is there any chance that I could come and visit you in a few weeks time? I'd like to scope out the property market in Bayfield."

Rose had a quick flash back to the previous year when, during her last visit, her sister and Lynda Forbes had become best of friends, almost to the exclusion of herself. She pinched herself to stop thinking negative thoughts.

"Of course, you can come anytime, just let me know when."

Rose put the phone down and let out a big sigh. Marriage split ups were rarely straight forward, and Kate and Bob's separation was proving no exception. In the end it always seemed to come down to money and retaliation.

Suddenly Rose paused as she recalled something Susan had said about Juliet's credit card not working.

Was money at the root of the murder of Juliet Carmichael? That was definitely food for thought.

SEVENTEEN

Susan had had a very restless night. Having combed through her notes again she still couldn't find any motive for murder. No motive and very few clues to why Juliet Carmichael was murdered. She absolutely hated it when a case went cold on her. *Please*, she thought, *let my team uncover some useful information, at least enough to get the investigation on a roll again.*

She poured herself a large glass of orange juice and then pulled out her iPad. Scrolling through her interview questions and answers from the night before when she had interviewed James Anderson, something niggled her brain and then she remembered the enigmatic manager of Ivy Cottage, Lydia.

Lydia who had supposedly witnessed Juliet making love at midnight in the sunroom with a mystery person. Could that man have been James? Had they possibly arranged a secret assignation, a clandestine rendezvous or had it been with someone entirely different? The smooth-talking doctor maybe, although he had said that his affair with Juliet was long since over. Who else other than James and the doctor could it have been? There were five other men staying at the farmhouse that night, could the mystery man have been one of them?

Susan could rule Tom Blair out or, here she paused, maybe not. He had admitted to being attracted to Juliet. But no, Tom wouldn't blatantly make love to someone whilst Rose was asleep upstairs. Susan scrolled through the list of the other four husbands on the retreat and read each of their statements. Not one single one stood out as even knowing the deceased.

So, it came down to Harry Carmichael, Dr. Seb Miller, James Anderson, or someone else completely off their radar. She would have to go back and interview James again and this time she would pull no punches and ask some more searching questions.

After a quick breakfast Susan decided to forgo her run. She decided she would catch James before he went to work. It was only seven thirty and she had checked online to see that his office was not open until eight thirty. *There would be enough time to interview him before he set off for work*, she thought.

It was a miserable looking morning, grey and wet. The lake looked menacing with white caps lacing across muddy green waters. Susan shuddered. Considering it was summer it felt more like winter. She wished that she had put on a jacket instead of her thin, silk blouse.

Driving up Highway 21 Susan passed the turn off for Cut Line. Dr. Ian Green's mother's egg farm was located somewhere off Cut Line. She remembered the lovely trays of fresh eggs that Ian had dropped off that previous summer when they were investigating the murders at The Little Inn.

She had so enjoyed his company, and then, unbidden, an image of Tone, the biker, flashed through her mind and Susan found herself feeling quite flushed at the mere thought of the bad boy.

What is wrong with me, she thought, although she already knew the answer. *I'm searching for love or is it just sex,* she reasoned. Oh, heck, it was both. Since the death of her fiancé, Henri le Bruin, four years ago, Susan's heart had been crushed. She had only started to date again a couple of years ago, but nothing or no one could compare to Henri. *Maybe,* Susan thought, *that was all Juliet wanted, simply to be loved.*

She pulled up outside the neat red bricked, turn of the century home belonging to James Anderson. Susan could see where the tornado had run amok through several houses on the street. New roofs and some complete new builds graced the road. It seemed almost impossible to imagine or even remember the devastation the tornado had wreaked on Goderich, particularly around the Square. Now beautiful mature trees swayed in the breeze, all the re-builds and renovations had long since taken place, and to a newcomer they would never know that a tornado had struck just six years ago on that fateful Sunday afternoon in August 2011.

Susan knocked on the door. There was no reply and no sign of life although James' car was still parked in the driveway. She looked at her watch. *It was only seven fifty a.m., and he should not yet have left for his office,* she thought. Susan walked around to the back of the house and peered through the glass panes of the back door. No lights on and once again no sign of life. Maybe he had gone for a walk, she thought returning to her car. She would go and pick up a Tim Horton's coffee and then drive to his chiropractic office and highjack him there, Susan thought as she jumped into her car.

There was a long line up for the drive through and so Susan parked her car and went inside. Tim Horton's was doing a brisk trade. *I should have bought shares in them years ago,* Susan mused as she finally reached the counter and was able to place her order for a medium coffee with double cream and a Boston cream doughnut. She sat at a small table tucked into the corner of the busy room. Picking up a copy of The Globe and Mail, Susan started to scan through the articles. It was a rare treat for her to make time to sit and read a newspaper.

Usually she would glance at the online CBC news if she had a spare moment. When Peter Joyce used to spend his weekends with her in Bayfield he would always buy the Sunday papers and they would lie lazily in bed and devour them whilst drinking gallons of coffee.

Susan scanned down the page and there, to her amazement was the headline, "Body found at couples retreat." She had known that the papers were onto the murder, but it quite surprised her that this case would make front page news. She would have to warn her team to be super careful of who they spoke to as many a case had been severely compromised by overzealous paparazzi spilling the beans too soon.

Glancing at the clock hanging on the wall over the counter, Susan quickly gulped down the last of her coffee and stuffed the Boston cream into her mouth. She decided to visit the washroom first before heading out and was pleased that she had, as looking in the mirror she found chocolate smothered around the edges of her mouth. She washed it off and combed her hair.

Jumping into her Porsche, Susan drove the short distance to the Square and parked directly in front of Anderson's office. There was a light on in the front office and so Susan opened the door and walked in. A young woman sat at a reception desk, phone in hand while tapping the desk with her fingers. She was clearly rather agitated. Putting down the phone she asked Susan, "Do you have an appointment with Dr. Anderson?"

Susan said no and asked when he would be coming in as it was already 8:40 and there still was no sign of James.

"I don't understand it," the receptionist said, "he is always here long before I get in. I've never known him to be late. He has a client at eight fifty, another at ten, and others booked throughout the day. He's usually so punctual."

Susan began to feel alarmed. Maybe she should go back to his house and see if he was there after all.

"Look, I'll go around to his house and see if he's sick or something." With that and with a deep, dark foreboding over-shadowing her, Susan drove back to the East Street house.

This time, after knocking loudly for a good few minutes, Susan went around to the back door and, using her credit card, managed to release the lock and open the back door. Entering the kitchen, Susan noticed immediately the remains of what looked like James' dinner by the sink and a half-drunk glass of wine left on the countertop. Nothing had been cleaned away.

She walked through to the hallway and paused. There was a complete stillness in the air which made the hairs on the back of her neck stand up. Susan walked into the living room and that is where she found him. Lying face down on the hearth rug, James neck had been twisted to an unnatural angle almost identically to that of Juliet Carmichael. There looked like there had been no struggle, just a twisted, broken neck.

Susan picked up the phone and made the necessary calls. The peacefulness of East Street would soon be shattered when the police arrived and SOC teams got down to their gruesome task. Another murder, another crime to solve, yet this one she would like to bet had all the signatures of the first. They were, in all likelihood, going to be looking for the same killer.

Standing in the hallway waiting for the SOC team to arrive, Susan closed her eyes and tried to visualize how the murder might have taken place. The fact that James Anderson's body had been found in the living room told Susan that he probably had opened the front door to a visitor, invited the person in, and maybe suggested that they go into the living room. This indicated that he might have known his killer, as people generally didn't invite strangers into their homes. The murderer would have followed James into the room and then come up from behind, grabbed his neck in both hands, and pushed his knee into his back whilst twisting James neck. He would have died instantly.

Retracing her steps back to the kitchen, Susan once again looked at the dirty plate with a knife and fork resting on it, and the glass of wine with only half the contents gone. Most likely, James had been interrupted from finishing his wine by a visitor knocking on the front door. What time was it when she had left him last night, Susan thought as she pulled out her iPad and scrolled through her interview notes.

Yes, she had arrived at his house at eight thirty, conducted her interview and was out and back on the road and home by nine o'clock. He must have grabbed a bite to eat and poured himself out a glass of wine just after she had gone, unless of course, he had eaten before she arrived, but no, he had said that he had been at the curling match before she phoned. So, if he had made his dinner, eaten it and half drank his wine after she left, the killer could have arrived around 9:15, putting the time of his death somewhere in the region of nine fifteen to ten p.m.

Susan sighed. Forensics would be able to give her a more accurate time of death she was sure, although by her reckoning, her timeline felt right.

EIGHTEEN

It was unusual for Rose and Tom to spend a whole day cooped up in their house together. The weather was so foul that neither of them wanted to venture outside. Puff and Ben both shared the same sentiments, one look at the rain had sent them both back to Rose and Tom's bed where they remained curled up on their duvet. They finally got up and had breakfast, then Tom made a bee line for his study leaving Rose in the kitchen pondering what she would cook for their lunch and dinner that day.

Although Tom had suggested earlier that they go for lunch in Goderich, the weather was so wet and miserable that neither of them fancied going shopping in the rain, even with the incentive of lunch. Instead they decided to stay put in their cosy home and weather out the storm together.

Pulling out the ingredients to make a marmalade cake, Rose proceeded to embark upon a cooking spree. She would cook pork chops with thyme and apple for their dinner and make a hearty vegetable soup for their lunch. Baking always helped her relax and gave her time to think and Rose had much to think about.

"A penny for your thoughts, love?" Tom said while coming up behind and wrapping his arms around her, "you seemed miles away."

Rose smiled at Tom, "I was just thinking about Juliet and Harry. Do you think that he murdered her, Tom?"

"I seriously don't know, love, but if he didn't, then who on earth did?"

"Well, there is James, although he did seem to genuinely love her and why would he kill the one he loved?"

"If I was Harry I wouldn't be killing my wife, I'd go after James."

"So, Juliet was stuck in the middle between the two men, both of whom claimed to love her." Rose said thinking as much out loud as anything else. "But what if there was a third person, someone at the couple's retreat who might have hated her enough to kill her?"

"You, love, were probably the only person to have seen this mystery person and you say that you're pretty certain that it wasn't Harry. Could it have been James?"

"Oh, Tom, I've thought about that and I really don't know. James is much slighter than Harry and the person I saw was slimmer and shorter, but I can't be sure at all. You know something, Tom, I really ought to let Susan know about my conversation with James, the one I had last night at the curling competition. I'll give her a call right away while it's still in my mind."

Rose picked up her phone and tapped in Susan's number. It was picked up straight away by a very agitated Susan.

"DCI Parker speaking."

"Oh, hi Susan, it's Rose. Look, I just wanted you to know

that I had a conversation with a man called James Anderson. He was apparently having an affair with Juliet Carmichael. I met him last night at the curling club."

"What time was it that you had this conversation with James?" Susan asked.

"It must have been around eight o'clock, maybe a bit earlier. We were watching the curling championships and, that was the other thing I wanted to mention. Harry Carmichael is on the curling team and he was not exactly behaving like a grieving widower, quite the opposite in fact."

Susan interrupted Rose quite sharply. "So, what was it you actually wanted to tell me about James?"

"Umm... I'm sorry, I got distracted. Yes, well, James told me all about his feelings for Juliet. He is really convinced that Harry killed her. He did appear to be sincerely cut up, a lot more than Harry. Did you know that James' sister is Sonja, Dr. Miller's wife?'

Susan didn't like to tell Rose that she already knew all about James. It still never ceased to amaze her how Rose seemed to find out information from people almost as quickly as the police connected to the investigation.

"Rose, I shouldn't tell you this, but you'll probably find out soon enough anyway, James Anderson has been found murdered this morning. We believe that it happened sometime last night. I'm at the scene of the crime right now and I'd better go. I'll speak to you later."

Rose stood in the kitchen quite still, barely comprehending what her friend had just said. Another murder, surely not, and why? And then she had a flashback to the heartbroken James pouring out his grief to her at the curling club. Who would want to kill such a sensitive man who she felt wouldn't harm a soul?

Tom looked up and saw his wife just standing very still. "Are you alright, love?"

Rose shook her head and let out an involuntary sob, "Oh, Tom, there's been another murder. That poor man I was talking to at the curling club, James, has been found murdered. What is going on here, Tom? It frightens me."

NINETEEN

Susan felt drained of energy and vaguely depressed. Finding a dead body was always a sobering event but compounding this was the unsettling thought that they had no leads to either murder. Hopefully her team might have uncovered something that might be able to kick start the investigation.

The team was already assembled in the Lion's Hall when Susan arrived bang on one o'clock.

"Good afternoon, everyone. We have some new developments to discuss. Some of you might have already read the dispatch about the murder of James Anderson. What you probably do not know is that I was the one who found him. I also think that I might have been the last person to have seen him alive."

Susan continued to relay to her team her interview with James from the night before and how she had returned the next morning only to find the man dead.

"It looks like he was killed by the same murderer; his head was twisted at the same ninety-degree angle as Juliet's. So, team, two murders, let's list the connections. Who would like to go first?"

Naturally Constable Ryan shot up her hand first. Susan looked around to see if any of her other officers might raise their hands. No one did.

"Yes, Constable."

"Well, ma'am, they were lovers for starters, oh, and isn't the Doctor's wife his sister?"

"She is indeed his sister, anything else?"

Susan had succumbed to the traditional method using the Lion's Hall chalk board. She wrote:

1. *James and Juliet – lovers*
2. *James brother of Sonya.*

Constable Elliot put up his hand.

"Yes, Constable, please go ahead."

"Wasn't James a member of the curling club?"

"Yes, you're right, and of course Juliet's husband is also a member. In fact, I believe that is how James met Juliet, at the curling club."

Susan wrote on the board.

3. *Both member of the curling club*
4. *James met Juliet at the curling club.*

Constable Brown put up his hand.

"Yes, Constable, what have you to add?"

"Didn't James recommend the couple's retreat to Juliet?"

"Yes, you're right although why he would want to encourage Harry and Juliet to get back together as a couple beats me. Anything else?"

"Sergeant Flowers put his hand up.

"James was slightly built. Didn't Rose Blair reckon that the bloke she saw Juliet with outside that night was slightly built?"

"Yes, you're right, Sergeant. It most certainly could have been James, although I think we can rule him out as the murderer of Juliet as he himself was murdered in the same way. Hopefully forensics should be able to confirm that assumption. Anything else?"

Constable Ryan put her hand up again. "Both killings, ma'am, have been executed with a degree of skill. Whoever has done them obviously has some military training, maybe martial arts, or maybe just a medical background. Up until today I had my money on James as the killer because being a chiropractor he would know exactly how to twist a neck."

Susan wrote on the board.

5. *Possibly James in driveway*

6. *Murderer's training could be medical, military or martial arts, trained to kill.*

"Thank you, Constable. The only two known people with medical backgrounds are the late James Anderson and Doctor Seb Miller. But we do need to investigate everyone's backgrounds to see if there is either a medical, military, or martial arts connection.

Constables Brown and Elliot, I give you that task. Right, let's be having your reports. Sergeant, you can go first. How did your interview with the not so grieving widower go?"

Sergeant Flowers stood up and scrolled through his notes on his iPad.

"Okay, when I interviewed Harry he was heading out for a business meeting. My overall impression was that he was impatient to get me out of his office as soon as possible. I asked him directly if he knew that his wife had a drug problem.

"At first, he flatly denied all knowledge and then I had to

remind him that we would be getting search warrants to search his house and bank accounts and that we would most certainly uncover any evidence of Juliet's cocaine use. I suggested that it would be far better if he came clean and told me the truth. After that he backed down and spilt the beans. Apparently, Juliet has been addicted to drugs ever since he first met her.

"First, she was a pot user and then she got introduced to cocaine. Her habit was costing them a fortune. He had tried multiple occasions to break her addiction by sending her to rehab programmes; the last being to Rice Lake where he thought they had succeeded, but then she caved in and was back on drugs within weeks.

"When I asked if he knew who her supplier was he looked a bit shifty. When I pushed him further, he said that all that he knew was that at least once a month Juliet would drive to Elora and when she came back his bank account was always a couple of grand lighter. He thought from bits of conversations he had overheard that her supplier might have been had a Mennonite connection. That's all I have, ma'am."

"Thank you, Sergeant."

Susan wrote on the board,

7. *Possible Mennonite connections*

"Team, we need to look into James and Dr. Miller's backgrounds to see if there are any Mennonite connections. Look, it doesn't automatically follow that the drugs or the drug dealer has anything whatsoever to do with the murders. We must examine every possibility. Constable Ryan, what did you learn about drug trafficking in Huron County?"

Constable Ryan stood up and scanned through her notes on her iPad.

"According to the Huron County Community Drug Action Team, all the commonly known street drugs are present in Huron County and sadly, cocaine is becoming one of the most popular of the drugs. The reason why is that coke had fewer side effects than the other methamphetamines. Goderich has one of the highest rates of cocaine use in the whole of the county, where South Huron has a higher rate of heroin pills such as fentanyl. Perth and Huron County are considered the crystal-meth capital of Ontario with Seaforth, Exeter, and Stratford, being particularly bad.

As to the Mennonite connection, apparently a man called Abraham Harm from Leamington, Ontario started a drug running operation between Ontario and Mexico. He himself was not a Mennonite, but he had connections with them in Mexico. His son, Enrique took over his business, moving massive amounts of cocaine across the border. After some huge American drug busts, he is currently on the run using various aliases.

Now this is where it gets interesting. Harms used farmhouses, mostly Mennonite farms, dotted across southern Ontario. He used these farms to stash drugs and money and recruited local Mennonites to help move the drugs. From what I can gather, ma'am, the hot spots for drug trafficking are Listowel, Milverton, Milbank, and Elora; all towns with large Mennonite communities."

Susan interrupted her Constable, "Did you find any significant movement of cocaine around the Goderich and Bayfield area?"

"Nothing specific, ma'am, apart from the biker gangs out of London who are known to traffic in this area. I did speak to the drug squad in London and they said that they have been watching the Goderich area very carefully as they have noticed a huge increase of movement of cocaine. They will keep us informed of any breakthroughs when they come. That's all I currently have."

"Thank you, Constable Ryan, a very thorough report."

"Right, it looks like we still have a way to go, but my instincts tell me to keep following the drug connection. I want complete and thorough bio's done on James Anderson, Harry Carmichael, and the Millers. Where they were born, which schools and universities they attended, etc... See if you can find any Mennonite connections. Sergeant Flowers, I give you the task of researching these men.

Okay, I think that we might be getting a little closer. Good work everyone. Now go out and bring me back some results."

The team dispersed leaving Susan typing up her report to send to the head office. She felt a buzz in the air. The case was about to break open, she could just feel it in her bones.

TWENTY

Rose had been preoccupied all day. Even her baking session had not managed to alleviate her low spirits. Somehow the death of James Anderson had affected her far more than that of Juliet Carmichael. The whole thing reminded her of a Shakespearian tragedy, like Romeo and Juliet, the star-crossed lovers. The murders felt somewhat staged and almost unreal. The unrelenting rain hadn't helped her mood either, plus being stuck indoors all day.

"Would you like a glass of wine, love?" Tom had said breaking into her reverie.

"Um... well, yes, that would be lovely." Rose said trying to sound chirpier than she felt.

Tom hadn't seemed to have been affected by the death of James, although he had been noticeably shaken by Juliet's death. Maybe actually finding her dead had made it worse for him or possibly it was just the gender thing. Not that she had been attracted to James like Tom had been to Juliet. If anything, she had felt more maternal towards the poor man than anything else.

But still, who could have murdered the two lovers? Someone with a grudge possibly? A jealous lover maybe, or were both deaths purposeful executions? Twisting the neck seemed like such a bizarre way of killing plus the fact that twisting a neck required skill and strength. *Could I twist Tom's neck?* Rose thought, *I wouldn't be able to even twist a chicken's neck, let alone a human.* But that got Rose thinking two things. Firstly, could the killer come from a farming background where killing chickens was commonplace or was the killer trained in the art of murder?

There had been something very precise about twisting the neck, Rose thought. She looked down at her hands that had been sub-consciously twisting the tea towel around while she had been thinking. Rose then thought about how stressed her friend Susan had sounded on the phone. *I didn't even get to tell her the most important part of my conversation with James,* she thought, debating whether she should phone Susan again. *Maybe if I invited her over for supper I could then tell her everything over the meal.* Rose picked up the phone and called Susan.

"DCI Parker speaking."

"Oh, Susan, I hope that I'm not disturbing you, but I wondered if you would like to join Tom and me for supper tonight?"

Susan smiled. Rose was a great cook and she really could do with a good homemade meal. All she had in her fridge was a lump of hard cheese and a couple of yoghurts probably past their sell by date.

"Um... that would be lovely. Look, I'm just finishing up my

daily reporting, I could be around at your place in half an hour if that's okay. I'll bring the wine."

"Oh, I'm so pleased that you're coming. I've got some more information for you, but let's talk later. See you soon."

That was great, Rose thought, she had killed two birds with one stone, making her peace with her friend and being able to pass on more information. But better still, she would get an update on the investigation if she played her cards right.

Susan arrived exactly half an hour later with a bottle of Merlot under her arm. She greeted Rose with a hug. Tom came ambling over saying, "Don't I get a hug too?"

Susan laughed and hugged Tom. Immediately she felt the chemistry between them tingle. She stepped back quickly and looked away. *Does Tom know that he has this effect on me,* she thought guiltily.

"Um... something smells divine."

"Oh, it's nothing, just pork chops cooked in cider with apples and mushrooms. Come through to the sitting room, Susan. Tom, could you pour out the drinks, please?"

"I'm ahead of you, love." Tom said as he entered carrying a tray of drinks and some little bowls of olives and nuts.

"Santé," he said sitting down to face the two women on the sofa across from him.

"So, Susan, what's up?" Tom said.

"Well, this investigation has been unusually slow. We've never had so little to go on before, but I am hopeful that we might have turned the corner at last."

"Oh, before I forget," Rose interrupted Susan, "I never got around to finishing off the conversation that I had with James. I think that it might be pretty relevant to the case."

"Go, on then Rose, I'm intrigued," Susan said leaning forward and suddenly looking interested.

"Well, he told me that he drove out to the farmhouse late Saturday night and met up with Juliet. He might have been the mystery man I saw with her in the driveway."

"Or," Susan said, thinking out aloud, "he was probably the lover Lydia saw with Juliet in the sunroom. Did he say what time that he was there?"

"Who on earth is Lydia?" Rose said, "Oh and I think that he said he was there around midnight."

"Lydia, Rose, is the manager of Ivy Cottage, you know that rather strange woman always hovering around behind scenes. She apparently is responsible for the smooth running of all the retreats held at the farmhouse."

"Oh, I never knew that. But Susan, if this Lydia saw James and Juliet making out in the sunroom around twelve, surely he would not have still been there at two when I saw Juliet outside?"

"My guess," Susan said, "is that whoever you saw Juliet with that morning was the actual murderer. We can probably rule out James as the murderer as the method of execution of his death mimicked that of Juliet, which would lead us to presume that it was performed by the same person."

Rose sighed, "So, I suppose I haven't exactly been much help, have I? It looks like we're back to the beginning, the mystery man in the driveway."

"Oh, Rose, don't beat yourself up. If the tire tracks found on the road match those of James' car then that will at least eliminate the possibility that the murderer also came from outside. No, most likely the murderer was someone attending the retreat. We'll get there eventually if only by a process of elimination."

"Right, well, let's eat, dinner is ready, enough police business. Tell us all about your love life?"

TWENTY-ONE

WEDNESDAY

Susan woke to a beautiful, clear blue sky. She got up and decided to go for a run before having any coffee or breakfast. Running always cleared her head. Instead of doing her normal marina run, Susan decided to run into the village and back. She would pick up some coffee from Shop Bike and catch up with any village news.

Susan ran over the bridge and turned right up Short Hill onto Bayfield Terrace. Passing Rose and Tom's house she took the next left turn onto Main Street passing the Pink Flamingo on the left and Virtual High School on the right. Running past the lovely Little Inn, Susan continued on up Main Street until she came to the library. Here she stopped briefly and walked across the road to Shop Bike. Both Shawn and Leanne, the owners, were behind the counter.

"Good morning, Susan," Leanne said, "Do you want your regular?"

Susan always had the latte when she came into the shop. It was one of the best lattes that she had ever tasted and was always consistently good.

"So, how are things with you two?"

"We're just fine. I hear that you've been assigned to the investigation of the murder that took place at Ivy Cottage. Shawn used to live up in that neck of the woods you know."

"Oh, really, did you by chance ever come across a Doctor Miller, Shawn?"

Shawn chuckled, "Sure thing I did, we all heard about his polyamorous relationships. Lucky fellow having two wives. Hey, I didn't really know him in person, just by reputation."

"I gather that that he likes his women?" Susan said.

Shawn looked serious, "Yeah, well, he's a randy sod, his wives, what were they called, Deborah and Sonja, well, my mom would have a thing or two to say about those two."

"In what way, Shawn?"

"Considering Sonja was raised as a Mennonite you wouldn't know. They both were apparently great party girls, attending wild parties, participating in sex orgies the like of which, according to my mom, you would have never heard of before. Sonja would have been excommunicated from the Mennonite community years ago."

"They're not sisters, though?" Susan asked.

"Ah, no, but I do know that Sonja grew up on a farm just aside Elora. As to Deborah, I'm not sure. All my mom used to say was to keep away from them as she thought they were sex maniacs."

"Well, thank you, Shawn, you've been most helpful. Right, I must get going. See you both soon."

Susan gulped down the last of her latte and sprinted across the road and down Charles Street, turning right on to Louisa and then back down Short Hill, across the river and turned left past the Docks and then right up to her condominium. The Mennonite connection appeared to be the much-needed lead,

Susan thought as she stripped off her clothing and made a beeline for the shower.

TWENTY-TWO

Rose and Tom woke to the birds singing and a beautiful blue sky. It truly was going to be a magnificent day and Rose immediately felt one hundred percent better.

Karen Huber had phoned earlier to ask if Rose was going to the Coffee and Croquet session at the Croquet Club, as it was such a perfectly great day for a game. Rose had agreed, and Tom had said that he would take Puff and Ben for a much-needed walk. Rose fished out her white capris and white shirt. Club rules dictated that all members should wear white when on the courts.

Karen was waiting for Rose when she arrived at the courts five minutes later. "Shall we have coffee first or after the game?" Karen said looking bright eyed and eager to go. Rose was desperate for a cup of coffee since Tom and she had only had their morning cup of tea in bed. Because Coffee and Croquet started at eight o'clock, she had rushed out of the house minus breakfast and the well needed coffee. There were also cookies set out on a plate. Rose grabbed a couple and stuffed them in her mouth.

Margo and Sandy arrived and walked over to Karen and Rose.

"Are you two ready for a game?"

"Yes, please," Karen said.

Rose looked longingly at the coffee. *Oh, well, it will just have to wait*, she thought as Margo tossed a coin to see which couple would go first.

"Heads," Karen called and heads it was.

"Do you want to play with the blue or the black ball?" Karen asked Rose.

"Oh, I'd like to play blue."

"Okay, then let's get started."

Rose set up her ball and the game began. It appeared that both couples were evenly matched. In the end it was Margo and Sandy that won by just one hoop.

"Right, coffee time," Rose said marching towards the refreshments. Karen followed her and soon the two friends were talking about the retreat.

"Of course, you heard about James Anderson, Karen?"

"No, what about him?"

"Well, he was murdered a couple of nights ago, in fact, the same way as Juliet Carmichael."

Karen looked shocked. "You mean to say, Rose, he died the same evening as the curling club championships? Oh my God, how awful."

"Yes, well, I really quite liked him. He was a sensitive sort."

"Brian was quite close to James. I know when his marriage split he told Brian how lost he felt, lost and lonely. Oh my, I still can't believe that he's dead."

"Karen, do you know anything about James' private life? I mean, where did he grow up? What about his ex wife? Where was she from? Why did they split up?"

"Honestly, Rose, who, where, what, why, when; slow down. What's with all the questions?" Karen could see by Rose's face that she was serious. She bit her tongue and answered Roses questions.

"I'll tell you what I know and it's not very much. James and his sister, Sonja, grew up in a Mennonite community just outside of Elora. All I know is that both brother and sister broke away from this community and moved to London where they went to school. As to James's ex wife, I know very little about her. I think that they met when he was at university. I do know that they never had any children. She lives in Clinton. I think that she's a nurse at the hospital."

Rose thought back to the previous year when she had been a patient at Clinton Hospital. Had one of the nurses been James Anderson's wife? Not that it mattered. He was now dead, and she doubted very much if his wife had anything to do with the two murders, unless, of course, she had discovered that James had been having an affair with Juliet. But they had been separated for over a year now, why would she still be jealous of any relationship that James had?

"Just one more question, Karen, and then I promise I'll drop the subject. Did James's ex-wife remarry or anything? Do you think that she might have been still holding a torch for him?"

"I think that Brian saw her with another man a month ago in Canadian Tire so, no I don't think that she was holding a torch for him. In fact, it was she who left him, not the other way around."

"Thanks, Karen. Right, let's have another game. Margo and Sandy, are you ready to take us on again?"

The four friends grabbed their croquet mallets and headed out to the courts.

TWENTY-THREE

S usan got to the Lion's Hall a good half an hour before her one o'clock meeting. She opened her emails and found that the results of the tire tread marks and shoe print analysis were in from the SOC team. The car parked by the side of the road by the entrance to Ivy Cottage was most likely a Toyota Venza. No surprises there thought Susan as James Anderson drove a Venza. That neatly tied up that part of the investigation.

They now knew that James had met Juliet late Saturday night, after everyone else had gone to bed, for their sexual liaison. But would the shoe print match James'? Well, apparently the answer was a definite no as the print measured a size 9 and James Anderson took a size 11. So, it was unlikely that James had been in the cabin where Juliet was found murdered, Susan thought. A size 9 shoe was quite small for a man, Harry Carmichael wore size 12 shoes, what about Dr. Miller? She would have to find out his shoe size and soon.

Dr. Ian Green had also sent her a note saying that the approximate time of death of James Anderson was somewhere between nine-thirty and ten which, Susan concluded, fitted in with her own reckoning of his time of death. She was not prepared, however for the revelation from the autopsy that James was also a cocaine user. Large amounts of coke had been found in his nasal passages and on his finger tips.

The blood work would take another day at least but he concluded his report with heavy use of drugs underlined. *Well, well*, Susan thought, she had not seen that coming. Both James and Juliet were likely drug addicts. The SOC team would, she was sure, find any stash of cocaine that might have been hidden in James' house. Somehow the James she had interviewed did not jibe well with someone who had a drug habit? Once again Susan was faced with the question, what was there a connection between the use of drugs and the murders?

The final emailed report Susan opened was from the IT crew at their headquarters in London. She scanned the report and let out a gasp at the huge amounts of money that had been withdrawn from the Carmichaels bank account. Over the past year alone over $100,000 had been withdrawn. Would all of that have been used to feed Juliet's habit or was there something more sinister at stake, possibly blackmail or extortion of some kind? They would have to wait and see just how much James had withdrawn over the past year.

The team arrived, and Susan prepared to greet them.

"Good afternoon, everyone," she said as they all took their places around the large conference table in the centre of the room.

"Right, it looks as if we've found our Mennonite connection. The late James Anderson and his sister Sonja grew up in a Mennonite community just outside of Elora. They left the area when they were in their late teens and then moved to London. Now I also have had the results of the tire track markings found by the side of the road outside Ivy Cottage. The tire marks are consistent with those commonly fitted to a Toyota Venza. James Anderson drove a Venza so that pretty well connects the dots regarding James' secret rendezvous with Juliet late Saturday night at the retreat. The foot print in the old cottage, however, does not match that of either James or Harry Carmichael. We do not have Dr. Miller's shoe size yet, but I would be very surprised if his matched as the shoe print found at the crime scene is only a size 9.

"Dr. Green, the forensic pathologist from Goderich sent me his preliminary report on the death of James Anderson. The top spinal vertebrae known as the cervical was broken by twisting the neck to a ninety-degree angle causing instant death. Bruising between the shoulder blades consistent with pressure induced to the back indicate the exact identical MOD to Juliet Carmichael. Also, high levels of cocaine were found in his nasal passages and on his gums. Further blood work will tell us more when Dr. Green gets the results back from the lab.

"So, we have identical murders and our drug connection. Sergeant Flowers, what did you learn about Dr. Seb Miller, Harry Carmichael, and the late James Anderson?"

Sergeant Flowers stood up and pulled out his iPad. "Well, ma'am, you've rather pre-empted me with the Mennonite connection. The only thing I must add about Sonja and James Anderson is that their family have connections to one of the biggest Mexican drug cartels south of the border. Their father's uncle is one of the head mobsters. As to Deborah, the doctor's other partner, I did a quick background check on her and could find no direct Mennonite connection. She met both Seb and Sonja at university where they were all studying to be sex therapists. They became a ménage a trois way back then. I could find no drug connection either. As to Harry Carmichael, as far as I can tell he was not into cocaine and from all accounts he loved his wife, Juliet. He was, however, paying for her drug habit. That's all I have to report, ma'am."

"Thank you, Sergeant. Yes, it does appear that we have found our Mennonite connection and hence, a possible drug trafficking connection. But how does this tie in with the murders? Any thoughts, team?"

There was complete silence in the room while the team digested the information. Constable Ryan broke the silence by saying, "Ma'am, we have thought all along that the murderer was a man, but what if it was a woman? When you said that the footprint was small for a man I thought, well I take a size 9 shoe. Could our murderer actually be a woman?"

There was once again dead silence in the room as the team contemplated the implication that Constable Ryan had put forward.

"Yes, you're right, Constable Ryan, we have rather focused on the perp as being a man, but there is absolutely no reason why a trained killer could not be a woman. So, what other women have we got attending the retreat that weekend other than Juliet? There was Sonja, Lydia, Rose, Karen, Sandy, and Sheila, six women in total staying at Ivy Cottage, although we cannot rule out any other outsiders."

Constable Ryan shot her hand up.

"Yes, Constable Ryan."

"Well, what about Dr. Millers partner, Deborah? She wasn't at the retreat, but she is connected to the case as much as she is Seb's second partner, and what about James' ex-wife? There are two women who could possibly have a motive and be involved in this case."

"Good thinking, Constable. We won't rule out anyone

although we still haven't established a motive for the two murders. We need to look into the backgrounds of all of these women to see if one of them has a background in martial arts training, a military background, or medical knowledge, plus a size 9 shoe. Constable Ryan, I give you this task. The rest of you keep digging into the Mennonite drug trafficking trade focusing on Huron County. Sergeant Flowers, I would like you to arrange a surveillance team on Harry Carmichael and Dr. Miller. Okay everyone, same time tomorrow."

The team slowly trickled away leaving Susan deep in thought. They had made the classic assumption that the murderer had to be a man and, of course, it could still turn out to be so, but Susan couldn't help but beat herself up for not picking up on the gender issue sooner. *I'm so tired and hungry,* she thought, *it's time to get something to eat and then go home and put my feet up.*

Susan was about to drive past the Albion when she noticed several Harley bikes parked outside. *Could one of them belong to Tone,* she thought as she pulled up alongside the bikes. Walking into the Albion she immediately spotted Tone sitting up at the bar. This time, however, Susan took up a corner table and beckoned to the waiter to bring her a menu.

Tone had seen Susan arrive and enter the room. He couldn't help being attracted to the woman although he sensed that she could be bad news. She had somehow got under his skin and intrigued him. He was, however, playing a little game with her. Tone knew that Susan was in fact a DCI with the London Serious Crimes Unit. He had made a few enquiries about her at the head office. It transpired that she was something of a hero having solved more murders than anyone else in the division, almost single handily. She did, however, have a reputation for being a bit of a man-eater.

The rumours abounded about her various affairs, particularly the one with the CSIS agent Andrew from Ottawa, who was himself a married man.

Susan did not know that he was onto her and he wanted to keep it that way for a bit longer.

Her dinner came, and Susan tucked into it with gusto. Tone let her get half way through before sauntering over to her table.

"Well, well, who do we have here then?" He said and pulled up a chair.

Susan looked up and smiled. "Tone, nice to see you again. I thought that you were not coming back to Bayfield before Sunday?"

"Oh, I'm just stopping off at my favourite pub on my way up north."

"Where are you going?" Susan asked.

"I'm heading up to Elora."

"On business then?"

"Sort of, but what about you? You never did tell me your line of work?"

Susan thought about it. Should she let him know that she was a police officer? To a biker gang member, it would scare him off and so she replied vaguely, "Well, I manage a team of people. My hours are very flexible."

"So, you're free this evening then?"

"Um... well, I suppose I am free. Do you know the village of Bayfield at all other than the Albion?"

"Not really, I'd love you to show me around the village, but only on one condition and that is I take you out for dinner tonight?"

Susan laughed, "How can I resist such an offer. I'll just

finish off my lunch and then we'll go. You don't mind walking, do you?"

"No, I love walking. I'm ready whenever you are."

Susan finished her meal, gulped down her Guinness and prepared to leave. Her day had just got better, and she was due some downtime.

They set off at a brisk pace walking down to the end of the main street, past Virtual High School and The Little Inn. They continued down to Pioneer Park where Susan suggested that they walked down the wooden steps to the beach.

It was a particularly beautiful evening; the air was still, and the lake looked as blue as the Mediterranean. In fact, one could almost think that the beach was somewhere on the South of France or maybe Italy.

TWENTY-FOUR

Tone and Susan walked along the beach until they reached the pier. Several fishermen were out. The marina was looking jaunty with all the colourful boats lined up. They walked up to the Mara Street footpath and then turned off and continued up the steep trail through a tunnel of trees. Both were quite out of breath by the time they reached Bayfield Terrace.

"There," Susan said, "we've pretty well done a circuit. If we walk straight ahead, we'll be back on Main Street."

She looked at her watch. It was only six p.m. "You know, Tone, one of the best sights Bayfield has to offer is the magnificent sunsets. Why don't you come back to my place for an hour or so and then we could go out for dinner before catching the sunset at around nine p.m. What do you think?"

Tone said that he thought it sounded great and they both continued to walk in companionable silence back to the Albion where Tone had left his bike and Susan her car.

"Just follow me, Tone." Susan said as she got into her Porsche and started to pull away from the Albion.

They were soon parked outside Susan's condo. It was only then that it hit her. She was inviting a strange man, a biker at that, into her home. *I must be absolutely crazy*, Susan thought as she showed Tone the way to her unit.

Tone was himself surprised at Susan's invitation. He wondered how long he should keep up the pretence of being a biker gang member?

Susan showed him into a lovely living room with a floor to ceiling stone fireplace that divided the living room from the dining room.

"Shall we sit outside in the courtyard?" Susan said leading the way out to a small patio where a large hot tub took up most of the space. Two red Muskoka chairs were placed between a small circular coffee table and several terracotta pots were filled with gauzy red geraniums.

"So, Tone, what's your tipple? Beer, wine, or spirits? I've got most beverages."

"I'll have a beer, thank you."

Susan returned with a small tray containing an ice-cold beer for Tone and a glass of red wine for herself.

"We've got a couple of hours to go before the sun sets. Maybe we should think about going out for dinner although I have to confess that I'm not terribly hungry right now."

Tone laughed, "Yes, you sure tucked into that burger at the Albion like there was no tomorrow and I suppose that wasn't that long ago. Let's just relax and enjoy our drinks for a while."

"I tell you what, if you can take my cooking I could rustle up an omelette or something for you to eat or we could order a take out?"

"If you don't mind I'll go with your omelette. I just feel like something light myself. "

Susan drank down her wine and got up to go into the kitchen. Tone grabbed her hand as she walked by.

"Let me make the omelettes. I promised you dinner and I make a mean omelette, if I do say so myself. You just sit back and relax and enjoy this lovely evening."

Tone disappeared into the kitchen returning a few minutes later holding the lump of mouldy cheese that had been languishing in Susan's fridge for weeks.

"Umm...on second thoughts I'm going to pop out to the supermarket to get some fresh ingredients for our dinner tonight. I won't be long." Tone disappeared before Susan could say anything.

She lay back in the chair and let out a deep, contented sigh. It was so nice to be waited on. She was determined to enjoy every minute of being pampered while she could.

Tone was gone a good twenty minutes. When he returned he entered the house carrying two bags bulging with groceries.

"Dinner will be served in thirty minutes," he said while opening a bottle of Pinot Noir and pouring out a glass for Susan and himself. He disappeared back into the kitchen and returned carrying a bowl of olives and nuts which he left on the small table next to the chair Susan was sitting on. He left her relaxing on the patio while he got on with preparing their meal.

True to his word, half an hour later Tone called Susan to the table. Immediately on walking into the house, Susan could smell the aromas of sweet basil and garlic. Sitting on the table was a dish of salmon poached in white wine, dill, garlic, and cream. Alongside the salmon was a dish of fluffy, creamy, mashed potatoes with a side dish of asparagus dripping with melted butter and a lightly tossed green salad.

"Wow, this looks and smells divine."

Tone smiled and started to serve out their dinner.

The meal was a relaxed affair. Susan felt as if she had known Tone a lifetime. She put it down to the fact that he was so laid back and accommodating. They talked about everything and nothing and yet there never was an awkward moment between them.

Susan looked at her watch and realized that they would have to hurry if they wanted to catch the sunset.

"Let's go, Tone, we've got about ten minutes until the sun sets. Leave the dishes. We'll do them when we get back."

The two of them walked quickly to Jowett's Grove and then took the small road down to the lake, where groups of people sat on the sand waiting to watch the sun set.

It was a truly magnificent sight. The sky lit up like an orange flame and then streaks of purple and red layered the horizon as the golden orb of the sun slowly disappeared and appeared to just slip into the lake. They were soon blanketed in velvety darkness. Tone took Susan's hand and together they walked back to her condo. Once they were inside, he put his arms around Susan and kissed her slowly and deliciously.

"I've been wanting to do this all evening."

Susan smiled and put her hands up to cradle Tone's face.

"Has anyone told you that you look just like Kevin Costner?"

"No, but has anyone told you that you're one sexy brunette?"

They kissed again this time more passionately. Susan could feel her body tingle with excitement. Her legs felt weak and suddenly she was consumed with such a desire to feel Tones body next to her that she fairly pulled at his shirt and ran her hands up his muscular chest. Susan could feel her breath coming in short gasps as Tone responded to her. He started to undo the buttons of her silk shirt as Susan in turn tugged at his pants.

"Oh God I want you, Tone, please take me now."

They made deep and passionate love on the rug in front of the stone fireplace. Their bodies fit perfectly together like a jigsaw and everything about their love making felt perfectly right. *How could this feel so good when I barely know the man*, Susan thought as she groaned out loudly. Tone was massaging her body and had just reached her g spot. *Just how many times can this man bring me to this ecstasy*, she thought as a ripple of pure pleasure coursed through her body. Tone let out a groan as his body shuddered and released. He wrapped his strong arms around Susan and pulled her tightly against his chest. He whispered in her ear, "I love you, Detective Parker."

Susan jolted away from him and tried to pull herself up.

"How do you know that I'm a detective?" she whispered.

"Oh, I know an awful lot more about you, but tell me, what do you know about me?"

Tone had propped himself up against the sofa. His naked body glistened with sweat. He stretched out his hand to reach Susan who had backed away from him. He could see that she was visibly shaken and was undecided what to do next. For once Susan appeared almost speechless.

"Umm... I don't really know anything about you other than the fact that you're a biker and a member of the London biker gang. Oh, and you have a wife."

Here Susan's voice wavered. She did not want to have a relationship with a married man, indeed, she had vowed never to embark upon another such relationship again.

Tone said quietly, "My wife died of cancer three years ago, so I am technically no longer a married man. I've just had the most amazing sex with the most beautiful and intriguing woman that I've ever met, and I cannot keep up the deception. You see, Susan, I'm on the drug squad, an undercover operative. I've managed to secure the trust of the biker gang and am pretty close to smashing open a drug ring that's been going on for years between drug mules in Elora and the gang mobsters in London. I've been undercover now for over a year and you're the only person that knows about my cover so please keep it to yourself."

Susan let out a huge sigh of relief. "And here I was thinking that you were a scary biker about to murder me. Oh Tone, you really had me frightened."

Tone pulled Susan to his chest and started to slowly and passionately kiss her. Their bodies moved together rhythmically, and this time Susan sat astride Tone and rode him like a magnificent stallion. Afterwards they collapsed, their bodies spent. Susan closed her eyes and suddenly felt sleep embrace her.

"Let's go to bed," she said huskily to Tone.

They went upstairs to Susan's bedroom and collapsed onto her bed, utterly exhausted from their love making. Tomorrow would be another day, they could talk then.

TWENTY-FIVE
THURSDAY

Rose and Tom awoke once again to the sounds of summer. Birds singing in the trees, a soft breeze blowing gently as the sleepy village of Bayfield woke up to a lovely summer's day.

Rose padded into the kitchen and put the kettle on for their morning cup of tea. Puff and Ben ambled to the back door and Rose let them outside to their fenced in back yard.

She carried two mugs of tea into the bedroom and gently kissed Tom saying, "Tea's ready," and went back into the kitchen to let the two dogs back in.

Returning to bed with the now awake Tom, Rose said, "Tom, we could do that road trip to Elora today. It's a beautiful day and for once I've got a completely free agenda. What do you think? I've fancied going there for ages."

Tom gulped down his tea and yawned. "Yes, well I've got no plans either. That sounds like a good idea. If we leave straight after breakfast, then we can be there before lunch and home again in time to feed the dogs."

With their day planned out Rose got up and dressed

putting on light summer jeans and a bright red sweat shirt. Tying a colourful scarf around her neck she then brushed her hair noticing flecks of grey coursing their way through her otherwise dark blonde hair. *I will have to start colouring my hair*, she thought and buried that idea along with any thoughts of dieting.

Rose and Tom had a quick breakfast of poached eggs on toast, fresh orange juice, and coffee. Tom said that he would take the dogs for a quick walk while Rose generally tidied up and cleared away their dishes. By nine-thirty they were on the road aiming to stop off at Listowel for a mid-morning coffee. They should get to Elora before mid-day in time for lunch.

Leaving Bayfield behind them Tom drove to Seaforth, on to Walton and then through Brussels, until they reached Listowel. As they drove, Rose realized just how rural Huron County truly was and she could well understand how over seventy percent of the county's economy was tied up in agriculture. There was, however, a new and burgeoning movement starting up in the County based on agro-tourism. Several micro-breweries had popped up over the county along with a couple of wineries and to her knowledge at least eight vineyards. Cheeseries, organic vegetables, herbs, mushrooms, and garlic were also succeeding in putting Huron County on the map.

The countryside around Listowel changed to hilly, rolling hills with Mennonite farms dotted all over the terrain. Rose counted at least half a dozen black horse and buggies on the road. She didn't know a huge amount about the Mennonites other than the fact that many had migrated from Mexico and others, like the Amish, arrived in Canada from the States and had settled in the rural areas of Huron, Perth, Wellington, and Grey counties. Just south of the village of Bayfield was a very successful Mennonite market called Zehrs and Bronson Line was home to a small Mennonite School and a little church. There were a few Mennonite families living on Orchard Line too.

Tom and Rose reached Listowel a little earlier than antici-pated. Driving down the main street Rose was amazed at how many shoe shops there were. Maybe they could look at the shops before heading out to Elora, she thought, but on second thought, decided against the idea. Tom hated shopping and it wouldn't be very relaxing for her having Tom pacing up and down while she attempted to look at shoes.

They found an old-fashioned fifties looking diner and took up a cubicle by the door. Ordering two coffees and muffins they found the staff incredibly friendly. Rose could see why the place was packed with people. *This is how the service industry should be run,* Rose thought while reflecting that many restaurants needed to take a few lessons in congeniality.

Soon they were back on the road again and entering Wellington County. Rose saw the signs for Fergus and Elora, and then they crossed the Grand River and she knew that they were close. There was, apparently, loads to do on the river; kayaking, tubing, trout fishing, and rafting, yet none of which however appealed to Rose.

She had, however, harboured a secret desire to have a go at ziplining. It had been on her bucket list for years, although Tom was not privy to this, and she was not sure if he would approve. The online write up about the Elora Zipline had made it all look very easy.

The zipline itself was set in the picturesque Victoria Park and traversed the gorge close to Lovers Leap just above the confluence of the Irvine and Grand Rivers. Rose had already checked out what time the zipline was open and how much it would cost.

She reckoned that if they got to Lovers Leap by two o'clock the whole experience would be over by two thirty and they would still have time to explore the shops and town of Elora.

"Tom, I was looking through places to eat in Elora and I found the Elora Brewing Company. It's a micro-brewery and restaurant. How do you fancy going there for lunch?"

"Sure, love, I'm always happy to try out some new beers."

"I think that we pass it on our left before the road goes down the hill into the main town. We're pretty close now, Tom, slow down or we'll miss it."

TWENTY-SIX

The Elora Brewing Company was nestled next to a collection of shops opposite the Elora Town Hall and very close to Victoria Park. It was all glass, wood and stainless-steel inside with the huge brewing vats placed at the back of the restaurant. It was packed full of people and doing a roaring trade. The menu was simple, mostly hamburgers and soups, pub food at its best.

Rose had picked up a brochure sitting on a table by the entrance to the restaurant. It was all about what to do and see while visiting Elora. She opened the brochure while they were waiting for their lunch.

"Wow, there's ton of things to do around here. I think that we will have to come back for a weekends visit. Look, Tom, there's a culinary walking tour and a farmers market every Saturday morning, oh, and a zipline in Victoria Park."

"A zipline? You mean across the gorge?" Tom said.

"Yes, it's run by an outfit called One Axe Pursuits and it's open now for the summer season. Oh, Tom, ziplining has been on my bucket list for years. I'd love to be able to cross it off."

Tom looked at his wife in amazement. "But you're afraid of heights. How could you possibly have any desire to be suspended over the gorge probably one hundred feet up in the air."

Rose said in a small voice. "But, it's a challenge, Tom. I want to try to conquer my fear of heights. I think that I will be able to do it."

"Oh, love, of course you will, but really, are you sure that you're ready for this challenge?"

"I won't know until I try, will I?" Rose answered and before she could say anymore their lunch arrived at their table. They both dug into their burgers and fries with gusto and Tom ordered himself a beer and Rose a glass of red wine.

"Well, here's to ziplining, love," and they toasted the challenge.

Parking their car by the roadside entrance to Victoria Park they started to walk through the trees towards the gorge. There were signs pointing to Lover's Leap.

"So, what's the significance of Lover's Leap?" Tom asked Rose.

"Oh, I read up on that. Apparently two First Nation lovers were denied marriage, and rather than face a life apart they chose to die by leaping off the cliff. A sort of First Nations Romeo and Juliet."

They had come to the sign that said, Ziplining Adventure – One Axe Pursuits.

"Right, love, are you sure that you want to do this? It's only $30 so it's not costing an arm and a leg, but you won't get me doing it. So, what's it to be?"

They had reached the zipline and Rose watched a man cross the gorge hooked up to a harness clipped to a wire overhead. Slowly he made his way towards them and finally he reached the platform. A man reached out to haul him in and for a few minutes the zipliner just stood there looking dazed. He was guided off the platform where he walked over to a woman who gave him a big hug. She was carrying a birthday balloon. The zipline experience had probably been his birthday present.

"Okay, I'm going to do it," Rose said bravely and walked towards the man in charge.

"I would like to have a go ziplining," she said. He nodded and handed Rose a typed-out disclaimer form which she filled out and signed.

"Umm.... it is safe, isn't it?" Rose asked with a slight quaver to her voice.

"Ah yes, look Miss, you're harnessed in and we pretty well haul you over the gorge and back. You'll be fine. Just don't look down until you're halfway across."

Tom paid the man the $30 and Rose stepped forward while the man in charge grabbed the harness and grappling hooks and attached everything to the overhead wires.

"Now, miss, hold onto this wire with both of your hands," he showed her a wire that ran parallel to the zipline, "and I'm going to start the zipline moving. You must move your hands at the same time, okay?"

Rose, up until then, had been too busy making sure that her harness was tight enough and that it was attached securely to the overhead zipline. It suddenly registered with her that she was about to step out into oblivion one hundred feet above the river. *I must be crazy*, she thought, and then she felt her feet drag beneath her.

"Hold the wire, love," Tom said anxiously as Rose's body was hauled to the edge of the gorge.

I mustn't look down, I mustn't look down, Rose thought,

and the next minute the ground beneath her feet fell away and she was suspended in the air like a rag doll with no control over her limbs.

"Hold the wire, love." Tom shouted and suddenly it registered with Rose that she needed to hold onto something. Grabbing the overhead wire, she was pleased to be wearing the thick leather gloves given to her and she felt more stable, although with her legs dangling into space she felt decidedly insecure.

Taking some deep breaths, Rose looked over her shoulder to her left. She could see where the Irvine River joined the Grand. The David Street West Bridge spanned the gorge in front of her. It had apparently been constructed in 1847 but had been rebuilt seven times since then. She was about half way across the gorge when Rose looked down. She gasped and practically fainted. It looked like miles down to the river. Her legs began to ache just hanging there and her arms ached too from gripping the overhead wire. *I've had enough now,* Rose thought and wondered if there was anyway of speeding up the process. Soon enough, though, she was being hauled back to the platform and it was with great relief when her feet finally touched the platform and she could stand even though she was still attached to the harness. Tom was there to hold her in his arms.

"Well done, love! I'm so proud of you."

Rose suddenly felt overwhelmed with emotions. Her legs turned to jelly, and she thought that she might cry.

"Oh, Tom! I did it! I really did it!"

Tom led Rose over to a park bench and they sat there in silence for a while. She took a deep breath and composed herself before being able to talk.

"Oh boy, Tom, that was scary, but now I can cross it off my bucket list."

"I don't know who was more frightened, you or me, love."

"I think that's enough excitement for me today. Let's just go into town and then drive home."

They spent the following hour just wandering in and out of shops. Rose could see that Tom was losing interest and so she suggested that they drive back to Bayfield.

"It is a lovely town," Rose said as they climbed into their car ready to leave Elora.

TWENTY-SEVEN

They had barely driven two kilometres when Rose saw a horse and buggy parked by the side of the road. A car was parked alongside. There was a woman and a man talking and it looked like they were having a big argument although Tom and Rose were too far away to hear what it was about. The man was obviously a Mennonite as he had a big, bushy beard, a black jacket, and wore a black hat. He looked like someone from a different century.

"Tom, slow down. Look, isn't that woman Lydia? You know Lydia, from Ivy Cottage. What's going on Tom, and what's she got in her hand?"

Lydia was holding a large bag and was in the middle of trying to hand it over to the bearded man.

"I wonder if she needs our help, Tom? Maybe we should stop. What if she's broken down out here? I don't like the look of that Mennonite. Come on Tom. Stop the car."

Tom pulled over and they both got out and walked towards Lydia and the bearded man.

"Are you alright, Lydia?" Rose said as they approached her.

Lydia glanced at Rose and Tom with a hard, steely look. Then, almost like the speed of lightening, she jumped forward and chopped Rose and Tom between their shoulder blades with the side of her hand in a classic Karate move. Both the Blairs toppled over like felled trees.

"Quick," Lydia said to the bearded Mennonite, "help me get them to the trunk of my car."

With much difficulty they carried the unconscious couple over to Lydia's car and unceremoniously dumped them into the trunk.

"We'll tie them up in your barn, Hank." Lydia said and proceeded to jump into her car while Hank climbed into his buggy and followed Lydia.

Hank's farm was just two kilometres down the road. The farm buildings had seen better days. Paint was peeling off the windows and siding and it was one of the off the grid properties with no hydro, gas, or mains water. There were two old, dilapidated, barns to one side of the rustic house. Lydia pulled up her car outside the farthest of the two barns. She waited for Hank to arrive in his buggy.

Pulling open the large sliding barn door Lydia peered into the darkness. Bales of hay were stacked around the perimeter of the building. Large posts and equally large beams crossed the rafters. Dappled light filtered through the outside barn boards.

Hanks buggy appeared at the top of the driveway. He pulled the buggy up besides Lydia's car and jumped down.

"I'll fetch some rope to tie them up. Who are they anyway?"

Lydia nodded and said, "They know who I am. They

could ruin this operation. Let me think, Hank. This is pretty serious."

"We'll get them into the barn, tie them up, and then decide what to do with them next."

"Okay, let's get them out of the trunk. They should still be unconscious which will make it easier to move them."

Half an hour later Rose and Tom were trussed up like chickens tied up to one of the large posts situated right at the back of the barn. Their mouths had been gagged with some filthy rags Lydia had found in a pile on the floor of the barn. Both were still unconscious, although Rose was beginning to come around and Tom was stirring.

TWENTY-EIGHT

S usan had woken up that morning with Tone gently snoring beside her in the bed. She was able to study him as he slept and liked what she could see. In repose, Tone looked younger, less craggy, and not such a bad boy. He still reminded her of Kevin Costner although an older version of the star. She traced his tattoo that ran across his shoulder blades and ran her fingers through his tousled hair. Tone opened his eyes and smiled.

"Good morning, sunshine," Susan said, "coffee or tea for you?"

"I'm a tea man in the morning, if you please." Tone said propping himself up on one elbow and eyeing Susan as she pulled on her baggy t-shirt which served as her nightie.

"We do need to talk, Tone." Susan said, and he nodded, "Let me have my tea first, my lovely."

Susan padded downstairs to the kitchen. Her mind had been on overdrive ever since Tone had dropped his bombshell. If he was an undercover cop with the Serious Crimes Drug Squad, might he also hold the key to the Mennonite connection which held the key to the whole murder investigation? She felt a little tingle of excitement. Tone might really help their enquiry and hopefully be able to fill in some of the missing parts of the jigsaw.

She made the tea and carried the two mugs back upstairs. Tone looked as if he had gone back to sleep until after Susan had placed the mugs down on the bedside table. He suddenly shot out his hand and grabbed her pulling her down onto the bed next to him. "How about some breakfast?" He said as he almost crushed Susan to his chest and began stroking her back.

"I want to devour every part of you," he said and lifted Susan's t-shirt, he began to kiss her breasts, her stomach, and then he buried is face into her very private parts and concentrated on devouring her there until Susan let out an involuntary groan. "Don't stop, keep going, deeper." She moaned and soon Tone was on top of her and their bodies joined together once more in pure ecstasy. Half an hour later they both lay sweaty and exhausted. Susan looked at her watch. It was already nine o'clock.

"Tone, didn't you say something about going to Elora today? You know it's nine. What time was your meeting?"

Tone smiled his lazy, seductive smile and said, "Actually, I don't have to be there until this afternoon. If my snitch is right, and he had better be as I paid him enough, the drop is supposed to take place mid-afternoon. I want to stake out the farm a good hour beforehand, so, really, if I leave here around mid day I should have plenty of time."

"So, Tone, are you going to tell me what or whom you're onto? It could have a bearing on the case I am working on and it could be helpful to know what it is that you're up to?"

"It's complicated, Susan, but I'll try to précis everything. As you are already aware, most of the biker gangs are involved in drug trafficking to some extent and this has been going on for years. While we have managed to successfully shut down some movement of the drugs, it is the suppliers that we are after and that's where I come in.

We know that the Mexican cartel has been sending up vast quantities of cocaine by multiple carriers. There has been, however, one central location that all the mules have ended up delivering their loads. This is a Mennonite farm just outside Elora. The mules or carriers bring up the cocaine from Mexico in relatively small packages. They keep them stashed away in multiple small Mennonite farms all over Southwestern Ontario. We have identified a woman who drives around to all these farms and picks up their stash. She then brings it all up to this one farm near Elora where it gets bagged up and then distributed to the biker gangs. This takes place roughly once a month, hence my visit today."

Susan interrupted Tone, "So, who is this woman?"

"Her real name is Lydia Klassen. Her cousin, Franz Klassen, was caught smuggling coke into Canada from Mexico in 2016. We've been watching her movements very carefully, monitoring her monthly visits to the mule farms. I hope today to actually catch her openly handing over all the stash to the Mennonite farmer, Hank Wiebe."

Susan was silent while she digested what Tone had told her and the implications that it bore on her case.

"This Lydia Klassen, Tone, might also be the same person we're looking for in connection to the two murders we've been investigating. I have one of my officers checking up on her background, but you probably have a complete dossier on her yourself. Maybe you could answer this question. Does she to your knowledge have any training in the martial arts or any military training. I ask because our killer used a very specific method of twisting the neck to kill our victims. Only someone trained in the art of killing would be able to perform such murders."

It was Tone's turn to go silent on Susan as he thought through what she had just revealed.

"I do have a complete file on Ms. Lydia Klassen. Yes, you're quite right, she is a black belt karate expert, and she did her training in Indonesia where she studied under a grand master of martial arts. Why, however, would she be involved in your murders? Do you have any motive?

"As far as I can see, our Lydia has been involved in trafficking drugs for several years, but we have no record of any violent behaviour. She's a tough nut, but I didn't have her pegged as a killer."

"Yes, up until recently we had our killer down as a man and someone with specialist training hence my question about military or martial arts. It does look as if Lydia ticks all the right boxes, but as for her motive, we have very little to go on. Both the victims were cocaine users and one of them had a serious addiction. That appears to be the only connection between them; the possibility that Lydia was supplying their drugs."

Tone interrupted Susan, "But if Lydia was supplying the drugs why would she kill her paying clients? Unless, of course, they owed her money, but it still would be rather extreme to kill, maybe a warning, but not death. Other than the drugs, was there any other connection between the two murdered victims?"

"Juliet Carmichael, our first victim, was having an affair with James Anderson, our second victim."

"Did you say Anderson?" Tone said.

"Yes, James Anderson, a chiropractor. He had his practise

in Goderich. He had a sister called Sonja who is married to a Doctor Seb Miller. Why do you ask?"

"We have had the Anderson farm under surveillance for quite some time now. They're Mennonites you know."

"Oh, yes, we know all about Sonja and James leaving the Mennonite community. They would have been ex-communicated by the Mennonites. So, are the Anderson's a part of the drug ring?"

"Yes, just one of the many I'm afraid to say although we have our suspicions that they might be higher up in the chain. Now, enough talking. I really must shower and get ready. Why don't we go out for breakfast? When do you have your team meeting?"

"Oh, not until one o'clock and by then you'll be on your way to Elora. Yes, I'd love to go out for breakfast, and I know just the place. I'm starving!"

TWENTY-NINE

Rose opened her eyes. It was dark, but as her eyes adjusted to the sun light filtering through the gaps in the barn boards, she was able to take stock of where they were. She looked around at Tom who was slumped over still unconscious yet beginning to stir. They were both tied to the same post, but if she shuffled her body round they might be able to undo each other's knots. Glancing around her, Rose saw that they were in an old, musty smelling barn. She could make out hay bales stacked to one side of the barn and could hear the scratching sounds of rodents around them. She prayed they were mice and not rats.

Wriggling her jaw and pushing out her tongue, the rag stuffed in her mouth loosened. She bent her chin down so that it was against the side of the wooden post and slowly she managed to dislodge the gagging cloth from her mouth. With her gag removed she was able to whisper to Tom, "Tom, can you hear me, try and wake up."

Tom stirred and slowly opened his eyes.

"I'm going to try to grip the cloth covering your mouth with my teeth and attempt to pull it down. Are you ready?"

Rose twisted her body and head and just about managed to reach the rag that had been gagged into Tom's mouth. She gripped the cloth with her teeth and pulled it down.

"There you are, you'll feel better now."

Tom shook his head and sucked in a deep breath. "Thank you, love, but what on earth happened? One minute we were walking towards Lydia and the Mennonite man, and the next thing we know we're waking up inside a mouldy old barn."

"I think that we were somehow hit unconscious. I've got a dull ache between my shoulder blades."

"Yes, so have I, love, but why? We only stopped to see if Lydia needed our help and then all of this happened. I don't understand any of it."

"Neither do I, but I do know one thing, and that is we have to somehow undo these ropes because they'll be back soon, and I don't want to be around to see what they have planned for us."

"Can you reach my hands, love?" Tom asked plaintively.

Rose wriggled her body around further and managed to reach by really stretching her fingers, the rope that tied Tom's hands together. Working the knotted rope slowly, Rose loosened the knot and began to feed the ends of the rope back through the knot. Her arms ached, and her fingers felt chaffed from the coarseness of the hemp, but eventually she managed to get the knot undone and Tom's hands free. He quickly gave Rose a kiss and then concentrated on untying his legs. Once he was completely free, Tom undid Rose's hands and helped her untie her legs.

"What do we do now, Tom?" Rose asked.

"Well, we try to get out of this barn and make our way back to the car."

"Quick then, Tom, we need to leave as fast as we can before they return."

They both advanced towards the barn door. They had just reached it when Lydia's voice could be heard on the other side of the barn door. They stopped in their tracks and listened. Lydia's voice sounded brittle and hard as she spoke.

"What do I do with them now?" She was silent while whoever it was she was conversing with talked in a low almost inaudible voice. Rose and Tom listened intently.

"How do we feed them to the pigs then? I mean, it would be a really messy job to chop up their bodies into small pieces even if they were already dead."

Rose looked at Tom with her mouth open, she couldn't even whisper to him, but they both had heard the conversation and understood the grisly implications. Lydia's voice was heard continuing her conversation.

"Right, okay, we'll get them to you and you can dispose of their bodies. Their car? I'll get Hank to drive it into the barn and we'll dispose of that later. We'll be at your place in about twenty minutes. See you."

Rose and Tom realized that Lydia had been speaking to someone on the phone and she would be opening the door any minute now. They looked around the barn. The only place to hide would be behind the hay bales and they would only provide a temporary hiding place. Tom beckoned to Rose to follow him. They ran stealthily to one side of the barn and ducked behind a stack of hay. It appeared that they were just in the nick of time because the barn door started to slide open and light poured into the empty space. Tom reached for Rose's hand and squeezed it tightly. He whispered in her ear. "Hold on there, love. We'll get through this together."

Lydia and Hank entered the barn and walked towards the back of the barn where they had left Rose and Tom tied up. Lydia shouted, "Hank, they've gone, look they've untied the rope."

"They can't have gone far; my guess is that they are still here in the barn. You go that way and I'll check out over there." Hank pointed to the bales of hay where Rose and Tom were hidden.

"Okay, love, we're going to run for it. Run for the open door and follow me." Tom whispered and once more squeezed Rose's hand and tapped her on her shoulder. He began to run, and Rose followed.

Hank shouted, "Stop, stop."

Lydia sprinted towards them. Rose and Tom reached the sliding door and ran with all their might out of the barn towards the drive.

"Come on, love, keep going."

Rose could feel her heart pounding and her breath coming in short, painful blasts. If only she had gone to more of the fitness classes. She felt horribly out of condition. Tom grabbed her hand and almost dragged her along down the lane.

Hank and Lydia were not far behind.

"Just a little further, love, you can do it."

"Tom, I cannot breathe. Tom, I'm going to collapse."

"No, love, keep going." Tom urged Rose.

He could see the road, only another few yards and they would be there, but he could also see that Rose would not make it.

Hank and Lydia caught up with them and Lydia grabbed Rose, who was so exhausted that she didn't even put up a fight.

Hank caught hold of Tom and pulled his arm back behind his back. Tom kicked Hank furiously.

Suddenly, a tall man wearing a leather jacket and a biker's helmet appeared from the road. He held a gun in his hand and pointing it at Lydia and Hank shouted, "Let them go."

Hank let go of Tom and Lydia released Rose.

"You two, come here," the biker commanded, indicating that Rose and Tom follow him. They quickly ran over to where the stranger stood. He nodded towards the road.

"Get in your car and drive away as fast as you can. I have back up coming and believe me, you don't want to be around if we end up having a shoot out."

All the while the biker held his gun out aimed at Hank and Lydia.

Tom and Rose were frozen on the spot.

"What's your name and just who are you?" Tom asked shakily.

"My name isn't any of your concern. I'm with the London Drug Squad. Now move it, just go." He growled and looked menacingly at Rose and Tom. That was enough for them to spur into action. They reached their car in record time and jumped in.

Tom revved up the engine and they sped away. It was only then that it truly hit home to them how close they had come to losing their lives.

"Oh, Tom," Rose cried, "What was all that about and just who was that man? Some sort of vigilante or something?"

"I don't know but we're not going to hang about to find out." He said putting his foot hard down on the accelerator and gunning the engine. "Now, love, I want you to call your friend DCI Parker and tell her exactly what has just happened. Maybe she'll be able to enlighten us."

THIRTY

After a leisurely late breakfast at Renegades, Susan had kissed Tone goodbye and headed over to The Lion's Hall. She was forty minutes early for their briefing, but after Tone's revelations Susan had decided that she needed time to write everything up succinctly and to send a copy to the head office, to keep them in the picture.

They were closing in on the murderer who was likely was the elusive Lydia Thompson. What wasn't clear to Susan was her motive for murder? It might have to be extracted from her when they tracked her down and had her remanded into custody.

Susan looked at her watch. It was twelve-twenty, Tone would be half way to Elora by now, she thought, and with a bit of luck would be successful in arresting Lydia during his drug bust at the Anderson farm.

The team trickled in ten minutes later. Susan could see by the eager expression on Constable Holly Ryan's face that she had much to disclose to the team. She would let her Constable report her findings before telling the team about Lydia and what she had found out about her involvement in organised crime and the actions of the drug squad. She had promised Tone that she would keep his name out of it as he was anxious not to blow his cover. He had spent a whole year easing his way into the biker's world and he couldn't afford to lose their trust.

"Good afternoon, everyone," Susan said to her team as they settled into their chairs seated around the large conference table. "We have much to discuss, but, right now, let's be having your reports. Constable Ryan, what have you discovered about the women attending the retreat?"

Constable Ryan stood up and scrolled through her iPad until she reached her report.

"Right, ma'am, I did find out some really significant information. Firstly, we already knew that Sonja and James Anderson had grown up in a Mennonite community in Wellington County just outside of Elora, but what we didn't know is that the Anderson farm is currently under surveillance by the London Drug Squad. They have been involved in trying to uncover the trafficking of drugs, in particularly cocaine.

"The Anderson farm is one of the biggest pig farms in the area and the owners are well respected in the community. I also found out that Lydia Thompson has connections to the Mennonite community.

"She grew up in that same area and has also been under surveillance by the drug squad. My biggest surprise, however, was that I discovered that Deborah, Dr. Miller's other partner, dated James for six months after his wife left him. The other interesting thing is that Deborah and Lydia are good friends, in fact, so much so, that they travelled all over Asia together when they were at university, travelling to Vietnam, Cambodia,

Thailand, and ended up in Jakarta, Indonesia, where they both studied karate under a grand master. When they returned to Canada they both finished their degrees and the rest is history.

"The other women on the weekend that I investigated have no known connections to the Mennonite community or any known drug connections, other than Sonja who I have already talked about. That's all I have, ma'am."

"Thank you, Constable Ryan. I have some more to add to your detailed report, although I have to say that you have uncovered a considerable amount of information which I'm sure will help to build this case. I have heard, on good authority, that a drug bust is about to take place later this afternoon. Constable Ryan was correct in identifying that the drug squad have been watching several farms close to Elora, the Anderson farm being the most significant.

Also, it appears that Lydia Klassen is involved with the trafficking of cocaine and has direct connections to the London biker gangs. She herself has been under close surveillance for a number of months now and hopefully this afternoon she will be arrested and taken into custody for questioning."

Susan was about to continue her report when her phone rang. She could see that it was Rose Blair calling and normally she would have just left it to voicemail, and she almost did not take the call, but something intuitively told her that it was an important call to take.

"DCI Parker speaking."

"Susan, this is Rose. Oh my God, we've just had the most terrible experience..." Rose went on to describe in detail their abduction and how Lydia had been part of the whole nightmare.

"Susan, what on earth is going on? Can you enlighten me?"

"Rose just calm down. Look, it appears that you and Tom somehow got tangled up in a drug bust. Did you say that a man wearing a leather jacket and a biker helmet came to your rescue? Well, he's most likely one of the undercover officers from the London Serious Crimes Drug Squad. They were keeping the farm under surveillance and watching Lydia's movements. Were you at the Anderson farm?"

"Oh, no, but we were about to be taken there. It's a pig farm, isn't it? We overheard Lydia talking to someone about feeding us to the pigs." Here Rose's voice started to quaver as she relived the horror of it all.

"Look, Rose, I'm in the middle of a team meeting right now, but I'll swing by your place afterwards. When will you and Tom be home?"

"We're about half an hour away from Bayfield, just coming up to the Winthrop Line. We'll see you later and maybe you can tell us exactly what's going on?"

Susan put her phone down and looked at the team.

"It sounds as if the drug bust has already taken place and that Lydia Thompson and a Mennonite farmer called Hank Wiebe, are now in custody. We will get our chance to interview Lydia hopefully tomorrow. Have any of you got some suggestions for the possible motive for murder? Why would Lydia, if she is indeed our murderer, be prepared to kill not one, but two people?"

There was complete and utter silence in the room as the team digested the information.

Sergeant Flowers put up his hand.

"Yes, Sergeant." Susan said.

"If drugs were involved maybe Juliet Carmichael and James Anderson owed money to Lydia?"

Susan had reverted to the chalk board again and began to write:

Motives? 1.*Owed money.*

"Yes, that's possible, any other suggestions?"

Constable Ryan put up her hand.

"Yes, Constable."

"What if Lydia had the hots for James and wanted to get rid of Juliet because she was jealous?"

Susan thought that it was somewhat far-fetched, but she diligently wrote on the board:

2. *Jealousy.*

"Right, anything else? Come on team, let's brain storm. Get your thinking caps on."

Constable Brown, who rarely contributed anything, put up his hand.

"Yes, Constable."

"What if blackmail was involved? Maybe Juliet and James had threatened to give up their source of drugs to the police?"

Susan wrote on the board:

3. *Blackmail.*

"Okay, we've got so far, money, jealousy, and blackmail. All valid motives for murder. But why kill James Anderson as well as Juliet? Any thoughts?"

The team once again lapsed into silence. Constable Elliot put up his hand.

"Yes, Constable."

"Maybe James was just collateral damage. Maybe he just knew too much by association with Juliet."

Susan wrote on the board:

4. *Collateral damage*

"Yes, well, thank you Constable, anything else?"

Constable Ryan put up her hand.

"Ma'am, if James Anderson grew up in the Mennonite community, he could maybe be connected to all of the drug trafficking, him and his sister, Sonja?"

Susan was thoughtful for a minute before replying.

"You know, Constable, you might be onto something. Throughout this investigation all we seemed to have uncovered is the drug connection. James Anderson could very well be part of the whole business. We know that he was a user of cocaine. Yes, it does seem too much of a coincidence that the drug bust has taken place right in his old stomping ground. So, team, we're back to the drug connection again. I'm afraid we appear to be going around in circles here and I honestly think that at this stage it is all pure speculation.

"We will have to now wait until we've interviewed Lydia Thompson. I would, however, like you, Sergeant Flowers, to accompany me to Lydia's house. I want to conduct a search of her property as I'm sure the drug squad will have that on their agenda as well. The rest of you keep searching. We might have completely missed some vital clue.

"Constable Ryan, I would like you to go back to the Miller's and interview Sonja and Deborah once again. This time take the hard approach. Talk about the drugs and the Mennonite community and see how they react. Right, off you all go, see you same time tomorrow."

"Sergeant Flowers, you can come with me, we'll go in my car."

Sergeant Flowers hesitated. "Are you sure, ma'am? I don't mind driving?" He had once been in the same car as DCI Parker and had been scared out of his wits with her speedy driving.

"No, it's alright, Sergeant. Come along, my Porsche is waiting."

THIRTY-ONE

Lydia Thompson lived in Saltford, home of the pioneers of salt, Samuel Platt and Peter McEwan. Her house was a short distance from Ben Miller. It took Susan almost thirty minutes to drive there using the back-country roads to avoid bridge construction just outside of Goderich. She took Black Point Road from Highway 21 across to Highway 8, then through the pretty village of Ben Miller, and turning left onto the Londsborough Road and back down to Saltford.

Lydia's house was just before Samuel's, the boutique motel and restaurant. It was a comparatively modest house tucked behind a thicket hedge. It did, however, have a breathtaking view over the Maitland River. Susan paused to have a look at the panorama. In the fall, she thought, the scene before her would be spectacular, as there were so many red maple trees and sumacs.

Sergeant Flowers and Susan approached the front door and, of course, it was locked. Susan pulled out her bunch of skeleton keys and choosing one carefully she put it into the lock and wriggled it to and fro. She then poked a wire in the same lock as the key and twisted it. The door opened to her Sergeant's amazement.

"Wow, ma'am, where did you learn that trick?"

"Sergeant, when you've been around as many years as I have you pick up a trick or two on the way." Susan smiled at his astonished face.

Putting on a pair of gloves she motioned to Sergeant Flowers, "Let's go in, after you."

Inside it was impeccably clean and tidy. Lydia kept a good house, almost sterile with its neatness. They walked through to the kitchen and Susan began to open drawers and cupboards.

"What exactly are we looking for, ma'am?" Sergeant Flowers asked.

"I don't know exactly, Sergeant, maybe something relating to drugs or perhaps personal letters. I'm not sure. You take the living room and I'll go to her bedroom."

Susan walked into what had to have been the main bedroom. A queen-sized bed sat in the middle of the room with bedside tables on each side and table lamps upon them. A large, old-fashioned chest of drawers rested up against the side of the room. Susan made a beeline for that. Opening drawers, the same neatness was found as in the rest of the house. Even her undies and bras were placed in neat rows.

Feeling disappointed at having found no incriminating evidence, Susan made her way down to the basement. It was a fully made up area revealing a large family room complete with a giant wall-mounted television. This room looked more lived in than the rest of the house.

Susan noticed a large map pinned to the wall behind the door. Looking closer she realized that it was a map of Southwestern Ontario. On closer inspection, Susan could see coloured thumb tacks pushed into the map dotted all over the place. Tracing her finger from one thumb-tack to another she was able to track a route that ran from Sarnia to the outskirts of Petrolia, across to the outskirts of Watford, up towards Thedford, to Exeter, and then down to Grand Bend, Parkhill, Bayfield, Seaforth, Winthrop, Walton, Brussels, Listowel, and several more thumb-tacks outside of Elora.

Susan counted thirty thumb-tacks in total. Were these where the farms were located that Tone had said were the drops for the drugs in the cocaine ring? If so, it was a large area to collect, and if it was Lydia, she would have to spend a couple of days at least each month on the road rounding up all the bags of cocaine.

Taking out her cell phone, Susan took several pictures of the map. They would find no traces of drugs, Susan was sure, in Lydia's house. She was way too clever by far to keep them there. *No, Lydia Thompson,* Susan thought, *was one smart cookie.* And she would be a slippery eel to interview of that she was certain.

THIRTY-TWO

After calling for a marked OPP car for back up and sending Lydia and Hank to London for processing, Tone and his team drove over to the Anderson farm. They could smell the pigs from a distance away. The actual farmhouse itself appeared unnaturally silent.

They've taken off, Tone thought as they hammered on the front door. There was no answer, just an eerie silence.

"They've cleared out." Officer Hillier said as they peered through more windows.

"No signs of vehicles, just pigs in the barns. It's as if they knew we were coming." Tone said to his team. How could they know we were on our way here unless somebody warned them in advance? *Who knew their plans,* Tone thought, and then he remembered his conversation with Susan. He knew that she would likely have briefed her team on the impending drug raid. He had only asked that she not mention his name, but the implication was that someone on her team must have alerted the Andersons otherwise how on earth would they have been warned off?

Tone pulled out his phone and tapped in Susan's number. "DCI Parker speaking."

"Susan, its Tone. Look, I hate to tell you this, but it looks like you've got a mole on your team."

"What," Susan spluttered, "A mole, what do you mean, explain yourself, Tone?"

"I'm at the Anderson's place having just arrived here from the Wiebes' farm where, incidentally, I rescued two people, a woman and a man."

Susan interrupted Tone, "Yes, I know all about them. Rose and Tom Blair are friends of mine and were just acting as good Samaritans when they stopped having seen Lydia Thompson in what looked like an altercation with a Mennonite farmer. It was a classic case of them being in the wrong place at the wrong time. Anyhow, you apparently rescued them right in the nick of time. They were going to be shipped off to the Anderson's farm where, according to Rose, their bodies were going to be chopped up and fed to the pigs."

"Well, someone let the cat out of the bag because I'm here and it's like the frigging Marie Celeste with not a soul in site, just hundreds of pigs."

"Oh God, Tone, I'm sorry. I can't imagine who on my team would spill the beans. I've worked with them for years and they've always been one hundred percent trustworthy."

"Then, if it's not someone on your team, who else would have had the knowledge of the drug raid?"

Susan suddenly thought about her friends, Rose and Tom. She hadn't warned them not to tell anyone about their nightmarish experience. Maybe, just maybe, they had inadvertently mentioned the drug raid to someone who had a vested interest in the business.

"Okay, Tone, I'm on to it. But before you go, I have to tell you about our find at Lydia Thompson's house."

There was a moment of silence before Tone gruffly said, "You mean to say, Susan, you've already been into her house before we got to go in? I think that you've over stepped your mark this time. This is our case, we should have been first ones in."

Susan felt her face flush and her anger rise.

"Excuse me, officer, a murder case takes precedence over a drug raid and if you don't mind, we are professionals. We haven't disturbed anything. But I can tell you now that you won't find any evidence at all in that sterile house."

She pressed the off button and stood there fuming. How dare he talk to her like that, she huffed and then Sergeant Flowers coughed and reminded her that he was still there and waiting to leave.

"Okay, Sergeant, let's go, we're finished here for now."

They drove off in silence, Susan still feeling hurt and angry with the way Tone had spoken to her.

THIRTY-THREE

R ose and Tom had stopped off at the same diner
called, Diana Sweets, that they had visited on their
way to Elora.

Listowel was looking particularly pretty under the afternoon sun and deep blue sky. They were not originally going to
stop but Rose desperately needed to use the washroom and
Tom needed a cup of coffee. He wished that he smoked,
somehow lighting up a cigarette might have had a calming
effect on his strung-out nerves.

He had felt jittery ever since their narrow escape from the
farm. Of course, a stiff brandy would have been even better,
but he wasn't about to suggest that they find a bar in Listowel.

Sitting in one of the cubicles a friendly waitress
approached them to take their orders.

"What can I get you two lovelies?"

"Oh, just coffee, please." Rose said having returned from
the washroom. "Oh, my, I look a sight, Tom. I think that I've
aged fifty years from our ordeal."

The waitress looked up from wiping down their table and

said with concern in her voice, "Did you have an accident or something, ma'am?"

"Oh, no, nothing like that just a case of abduction and almost being fed to the pigs at a farm." Rose laughed almost hysterically. It had all sounded so bizarre and by the weird look that the waitress gave her she probably thought that Rose was on something, maybe drugs?

Tom smiled at the waitress and jokingly said, "Don't mind my wife, she's only kidding around."

The waitress nodded and, giving Rose another strange look, went to fetch their coffee.

"Rose," Tom said, "pull yourself together. You can't be talking about abduction and pigs to the locals. These small communities are almost incestuous, everyone knows someone who knows someone. That waitress could be calling up the Anderson farm right now as we speak."

Never a truer word had been spoken in jest. As Tom was dressing Rose down the waitress was indeed phoning her uncle, Jeb Anderson, who in turn would make several more phone calls to those above him in the drug chain. The wheel would be set in motion. The grand cover up had begun.

Rose and Tom got home and were greeted by two excited dogs. Tom grabbed their leashes and said that he would take them for a quick walk while Rose prepared their evening meal.

Neither of them was very hungry so Rose prepared a light meal of poached salmon fillets on a pilaf of rice. She put together a tossed salad and when Tom came in he opened a bottle of Chardonnay. They had just started their dinner when the phone rang. It was Susan Parker asking if she could come and visit them. She would be around in ten minutes.

"So much for a leisurely meal," Tom muttered as he hurriedly ate up his dinner.

Susan arrived exactly ten minutes later, and Rose could see from her body language that she was not in a good mood.

"Hi, Susan," Rose said, "do you fancy a glass of wine?"

"Umm...no, this isn't actually a social visit. Look, I have to ask you both, did you tell anyone about the drug bust or about your abduction?"

Rose hesitated before answering, "No, not really."

Tom piped up. "We were at a diner called Diana Sweets in Listowel and Rose made some facetious remark about being abducted and almost fed to the pigs. She was only joking around, although I think the waitress thought that she was being hysterical. The server gave her a very weird look and I just said that she wasn't herself. So, we didn't actually reveal anything about the drug bust."

Susan looked aghast, "What on earth got into you, Rose to even talk about being abducted?"

"Oh, Susan, I'm sorry. I suppose I wasn't thinking and I was just kidding around. You know how when you've had a bad day the best thing to do is to make light of it. I didn't say anything incriminating. I promise."

Susan's face softened a little, "Oh well, my friends, you might have just caused a big drug bust to go south. It's not your fault, just a set of unfortunate circumstances. Anyway, at least you're both not harmed. You do know that we're dealing with some dangerous people. I want you two to keep a low profile for a while."

"I thought that Lydia had been arrested?" Tom said.

"Yes, she has and is in custody in London, but we haven't interviewed her yet. Right now, she's been arrested for dealing in drugs. Hopefully we'll be able to pin her for the murders too."

"What about our abduction?"

"We'll see what we can do about that. Don't worry, we will be pressing charges. Right now, I must go, and you two look exhausted. Try and get an early night and I'll keep you posted about Lydia as soon as I can."

Susan left, and Rose and Tom gave each other a look that said we blew it. Rose then shrugged her shoulders and went back to eating her now rather cold dinner.

Susan drove back to her condo deep in thought. In some ways she was relieved that she did not have a mole in her team. However, it did beg the question about the waitress from the diner being an informant. They would be hard pushed to get anything to stick on anyone in that small community, besides she was probably related to one of the farm owners in the investigation.

She had just walked in and opened her kitchen cupboards to see what she could possibly find to cook for her supper and had discovered two tins of Campbell's Soup, when the door-bell rang. Opening the door Susan found a contrite looking Tone clad in his leathers, biker's helmet in one hand and a bouquet of flowers in the other.

He said in a quiet, meek voice, "These are for you, Susan as a way of apology for my bad behaviour earlier on. I just wanted to tell you that you were perfectly in your rights to search Lydia's house. Please accept my sincere apologies."

Bending forward down on one knee he handed Susan the flowers. He looked so ridiculous that Susan laughed out aloud.

"Oh, for God's sake, Tone, get up and give me a kiss. Just come in before the neighbours see you. They'll think that you are proposing to me."

"Well, I might just be doing that one day." Tone said and jumped up and grabbed Susan throwing his helmet and flowers onto the floor.

"Oh, I love a feisty woman," and then they kissed passionately and deeply.

Susan finally pulled away and said, "So, what's happening to Lydia?"

"The arraignment for her is set for tomorrow. I've booked the interview room for you for ten o'clock. We will have finished with her by then but if you don't mind, I wouldn't mind sitting in on your interview."

"Sure, Tone, thanks for booking the room. Now, I was about to heat up some soup. What do you want, mushroom or tomato?"

"I tell you what I want and that is you." Tone pulled Susan to his chest and held her so tightly that she could hardly breathe.

"Could we have some pre-dinner sex and then I'm going to take you out to dinner. I owe you at least a meal for my bad behaviour."

THIRTY-FOUR

FRIDAY

Susan woke up at six to find that Tone had already gone. On the kitchen counter, next to the kettle, there was a short note which thanked her for the most amazing night and that he would see her again at ten.

She looked at her watch and decided that there was enough time for her to go for a quick run before leaving for London. It should only take about an hour and a bit to drive there so as long as she left Bayfield before eight thirty she would be at the Serious Crimes Unit easily by ten.

Setting off at a brisk pace Susan decided to run across the highway to Old River Road and then up the hill. She loved that particular route, as it was so pretty running through a tunnel of cedar trees. When she reached the top of the hill at the stop sign she debated whether to turn right and run the Sawmill Creek trail or to turn left and do the circuit back to the highway and back down to Bayfield River Road. She decided on the latter and set off again at a goodly pace.

Ten minutes later, Susan was back in her condo and stripped down naked to have a long, refreshing shower. By eight o'clock Susan had made herself a pot of coffee, grabbed her coffee-to-go mug, hunted in the fridge and cupboard for something to eat for breakfast, and then set off in her silver Porsche to London.

It was a truly lovely drive with so little traffic on the highway that Susan was able to put her foot down and really give the engine a good run. She got to London and the Serious Crimes Headquarters in record time and managed to find a parking space in the underground car park. With twenty minutes to spare, Susan had time enough to find a Tim Hortons, grab a bagel with cream cheese and another coffee, and still be back at the office in time for her interview with Lydia Thompson.

Lydia was sitting in the interview room, a small box of a space which just managed to hold a tiny table, four chairs, and a wall-mounted security camera. The whole room was wired for built in audio-visual technology, no need for tape recordings as everything was high tech now.

Tone knocked on the door and entered. Taking a seat opposite Lydia and next to Susan, he sat impassively waiting for her to begin the interview.

"Firstly, for the record, Ms. Thompson is waiving legal representation. She has agreed to be questioned without the said representation. So, Ms. Thompson, before we start I wish to reiterate the following. You must clearly understand that anything said to you previously should not influence you or make you feel compelled to say anything at this time. Whatever you felt influenced or compelled to say earlier, you are now not obliged to repeat, nor are you obliged to say anything further, but whatever you do say may be given as evidence. Do you understand?"

Lydia agreed by nodding her head and then she opened her mouth to speak.

"I would like to know why I am here being interviewed by you, DCI Parker when I have already been questioned once by the drug squad and twice by one of your officers regarding the murder at Ivy Cottage? This verges on police harassment"

Oh, I just knew that she would be a slippery person to interview, Susan thought, and she knew her rights too.

"I am arresting you, Ms. Thompson, on suspicion of being an accessary to murder. Where were you on the night of Friday, May 31st and the evening of Monday, June 3rd?"

Lydia let out a deep sigh and said, "We've already been through this. Look, I was in my room at Ivy Cottage and asleep on the Friday night, but I have no alibi. I would also assume that none of the other guests staying at Ivy Cottage have alibi's either. No, I did not murder Juliet Carmichael. As to the evening of June 3rd, I really cannot remember where I was, probably at home in Saltford. I live alone so once again, I have no one to vouch for me. Is this about the murder of James Anderson? Why on earth would I murder him?"

"Umm... Ms. Thompson, what size shoe do you take?"

Lydia looked at Susan and pulled a face, "That's a funny question to ask, what on earth has my shoe size got to do with the murders? If you must know, I take a size 10, sometimes an 11 depending on the shoe."

Susan looked deflated. She said, "I have no more questions for you at this moment. Officer McCleary will be charging you with two counts of kidnapping and forceable confinement in addition to the current charge of drug trafficking."

Susan indicated to Tone that she was finished with Lydia and got up to leave the room. Before she departed though, she turned to Lydia and said, "You would be better off telling us the truth, Ms. Thompson, because it will all come out in the wash, believe me. Your dealings with the drug ring, who your immediate handlers are, your involvement with the bikers and the Mexican cartel, all of this, I promise you, will be uncovered; so the longer you withhold vital information from us the worse it will look on your sheet. My advice to you is, spill the beans now."

Susan looked at Tone and nodded her head and wiggled her fingers as a goodbye. If she left immediately she would be back in Bayfield in time for her team meeting.

THIRTY-FIVE

Rose and Tom had got up that morning feeling refreshed and ready to face the day with a smile on their faces. Tom announced that he was off to play a game of golf and Rose decided to get some baking done as Jessica, Rob, and the children were coming to visit the next day. She would make Abby and Ella's favourite chocolate cake, but what should she make for the actual main meal?

Jessica had announced that she was going gluten and lactose free so that immediately eliminated many of Rose's favourite dishes which used cheese and cream, pastry, or indeed any thickening other than rice, corn, or chickpea flour.

She opened the freezer to see what she had. There was a joint of beef; maybe a traditional roast, Yorkshire puddings, and gravy would suffice. They could have the cake for dessert and Rose would make a fruit salad for Jessica. With the menu all settled she was about to start on the baking when the phone rang. It was her friend Karen.

"Oh, hi, Karen, how are you?"

"I'm fine, Rose, but I wondered if you'd like to come out to my place for coffee this morning?"

Rose briefly thought to herself that she could delay making the cake until that afternoon.

"Yes, I'd love to. What time?"

"What about around ten-thirty?"

"Sure, that would be great. See you soon."

Rose put the phone down and went to her bedroom. When she got up, she had just thrown on an old pair of jeans and a tatty old sweatshirt. She should probably change into something a little smarter. Choosing a light summer dress, Rose quickly changed, brushed her hair, and put on some lipstick. She called Puff and Ben over to the back door and let them out saying, "I'll take you for a walk when I return, I promise. Be good dogs while I'm out."

Grabbing the keys to her old Volvo, Rose jumped into the car and drove out to the highway. Karen lived just south of the village down at Houston Heights. Brian and she had a sweet cottage by the lake. Their main residence was in Waterloo, but they spent their summers in Bayfield.

Pulling up in front of their house Rose was greeted by Karen.

"Come in Rose, I've set out our coffee around the back on the patio."

The two friends walked out to the back of the house and immediately the beautiful blueness of Lake Huron awaited them. *What an amazing sight*, Rose thought. *I would never tire of this view, in fact, I probably wouldn't get anything done as I would spend the whole day just viewing the lake.*

"So, how are things?" Karen asked.

"Well, Tom and I went to Elora for the day and, oh, Karen, I went ziplining."

"Oh my God, you did it? You actually ziplined across the gorge?" Karen said clearly impressed.

"I can't say that I'll ever do it again, but I can cross it off my bucket list."

Karen laughed and then changed the subject. "So, Rose, any news about the murders?"

Rose debated whether to tell her friend about the drug bust. After Susan's chilly reaction to her silly disclosure at the diner in Listowel, she hesitated. Karen could see her hesitation.

"What is it, Rose? Has something happened? You look serious."

Rose coughed and then sighed, finally saying, "I can't tell you everything, Karen, and please don't tell anyone about this, but Tom and I had a bit of..." Rose paused as she sought the right word. "Umm... we had an altercation with Lydia."

Karen interrupted Rose, "You mean Lydia, the Lydia from Ivy Cottage? What sort of altercation?"

"It's complicated, but I can tell you that she's probably the prime suspect for both murders."

"Oh my gosh, Rose. I thought that she was a strange woman, although I also thought that the other woman was weird too."

"Which other woman?"

"Oh, I think that she was a cleaner or something. I saw Lydia and her in the dining room deep in conversation and then I saw her go upstairs."

"Who was she?"

"I think that I overheard Lydia call her Deb. Does that name ring any bells?"

"No, but why did you think that she was strange?"

"Rose, I'm not really sure, it was probably just the way the two of them were interacting. I could tell through their body language, I suppose."

"I wonder if DCI Parker knows about this Deb woman? Did you mention it to her when you were interviewed by the police?"

Karen thought back to her chat with Constable Ryan. "You know, I don't think that I did. The questions she asked me were more about Juliet herself then anything else."

"Oh, well, it's probably not relevant anymore as Lydia is the prime suspect. Let's change the subject though, it creeps me out just thinking about that woman."

Karen laughed, "Did you say that your daughter, Jessica was coming tomorrow? How is she and how are those adorable granddaughters of yours?"

"Abby and Ella are doing well. They're both at French Immersion school now in London and can chatter away quite fluently in French. You know they're growing up before my very eyes."

"Yes, I know. I wish that my boys would give us a grand-child or two, but no signs yet of any interest in becoming parents. How many grandchildren do you have now, Rose?"

"We've got four and a fifth on the way."

"I'm so jealous," Karen laughed and the two of them chatted amicably for a while before Rose looked at her watch and said that she would have to get going.

"Thanks so much for the coffee, Karen. We must get together again soon."

Rose drove away deep in thought. Just who was this mystery woman, Deb?

THIRTY-SIX

Susan reached Bayfield with forty minutes to spare. She decided to grab some lunch at the Japanese restaurant, Drift.

Sitting beneath an umbrella on the patio she began to relax. The last few days had been very stressful, although thinking back to the delicious time spent with Tone brought a lovely warm feeling through her body. Susan smiled and closed her eyes and let the sun bathe her face.

"Susan, enjoying the sun, are you?"

She opened her eyes and there was Dr. Ian Green standing there with his funny lopsided grin plastered over his face.

"Oh hi, Ian. Fancy meeting you here. Are you staying for lunch?"

"Yes, I was about to order. Do you mind if I join you?"

"Sure, I could do with some company. I've just come from interviewing our one and only suspect and have realized that she couldn't be our killer. It's pretty depressing to think that we might be back to square one."

"Actually, Susan, there is something I had wanted to talk to you about. You will receive this in writing, but I'll run it by you now. I sent the cocaine samples from the nasal passages of both your victims to be further analysed. We have a new facility over by Woodstock where they can determine through computer analysis and comparison with our data base the original source of the drug. I think that you might be interested in the results."

Susan thought to herself, but did not say out aloud, *if only he wasn't so pedantic and serious. I could quite fancy the man.* She shook her head and tried to focus on what the doctor was saying.

"In short, your victims had inhaled cocaine grown and processed in Venezuela."

"Venezuela," Susan said, "Are you sure? I was convinced that this was a Mexican import."

"Ah, some drugs on the market come directly from Venezuela, Columbia, and Nicaragua and then make there way up to Mexico, whereas others are flown in direct from their original source. They tend to be the purest and strongest. The risk of multiple handlers in the drug business, is greed. Many stashes of cocaine get cut with other fillers, some of which can have lethal results."

Susan knew all about the spiking of drugs. There had, indeed, been many deaths among the London drug users and a disproportionate number could have been avoided if the purity of the drug had not been tampered with. But Venezuela?

Their lunch arrived and they both ate their meal in companionable silence. Susan looked at her watch. It was almost one and her team would be waiting. She opened her wallet to pay saying, "Ian, I'll give you this money to pay for my lunch. I really have to dash now as I'm already late. See you."

She headed out to where her Porsche was parked and ran head on into Tom Blair.

"Whoa. Slow down, Susan," Tom laughed as he held her in his arms. She had almost fallen over in their collision.

"Oh, sorry, Tom, I was preoccupied and heading out to my team meeting. I hope that I didn't hurt you."

Tom laughed again, "It was worth it just to hold you in my arms again. Anyhow, I must be going too, got a rendezvous at the Albion."

Susan reflected, as she had so often done before, that under different circumstances she could fall for Tom Blair. Without fail he ignited a flame of desire within her whenever they touched and right now being held in his arms was no exception.

Susan arrived at the Lion's Hall five minutes later. Her team were already sitting around the conference table talking. She rushed in.

"Good afternoon, everyone. Sorry I'm late but I came from London where I was interviewing Lydia Thompson. I have much to tell you, but first, let's have your report, Constable Ryan. How did you get on with reinterviewing Deborah and Sonja?"

Constable Ryan stood up and grabbed her iPad, scrolling through she found her interview notes.

"Sonja Anderson denied knowing anything about the drugs. She knew nothing about her brother's habits or Juliet Carmichael's drug addiction. She appeared equally ignorant of the Mennonite communities and their connection to drugs. I tend to believe her as she didn't appear to be lying. However, it was a different story with Deborah. Before I interviewed her, I ran a search through the Interpol data base on both women and this is what I found. Deborah Nock's real name is Isabella

Carbella. She is the great-granddaughter of the National Assembly President Diosidado. He was reputed to be the chief king pin of the Venezuelan drug ring, more commonly known as The Cartel of the Sun. This cartel is made up of many high-ranking members of the Venezuelan armed forces and they have strong connections to the Mexican cartel which operates under the name of Los Zebas.

Isabella, masquerading as Deborah, is wanted for trafficking offences dating back over ten years. She is believed to be the king pin of the drug market in Ontario. Isabella is also wanted for four counts of murder. She has a black belt in Karate and is known for her killer moves. She has appeared to have gone underground these past ten years. That's all I have to report, ma'am, other than the fact that when I interviewed her, she flatly denied any knowledge of drugs."

There was a hushed silence in the room before Sergeant Flowers spoke.

"We already know that Lydia and Deborah, I mean Isabella, are friends and that they both have black belts in Karate. It is too much of a stretch to believe that the one woman is a drug mule while the other claims to have no connection to drugs. Could the two women be working together?"

"Good thinking, Sergeant, but after my interview with Lydia Thompson today I tend to think that she is not herself guilty of the murders of Juliet and James. Apart from her emphatic denial of both murders which I tended to believe, the biggest piece of evidence that collaborates her denial is the size of the foot print left in the cabin. Ms. Thompson's foot size is 10 and the footprint found at the scene of the crime was measured at size 9. No, I do not believe that Lydia herself committed the murders although there is absolutely no doubt

that she is directly involved in the drug trafficking and by association may have knowledge of the murders. But here's the
thing, is she aware that Deborah, or Isabella as we now know
her, was the controlling king pin of the Ontario drug movement and does that have any direct bearing on the two
murders?

"So far, this whole investigation has revolved around sex,
drugs, and lies. We still do not have a positive motive for
murder. Right, Sergeant, I want you to come with me. We
need to arrest this Isabella Carbella before she gets wind of the
fact that we know who she really is and disappears. It's about
time that we got some truthful answers. I'm so fed up with all
the lies. Okay, Sergeant, let's go. The rest of you go home and
get some well-deserved rest. We'll meet same time tomorrow
and hopefully we might be closer to wrapping up this frus-
trating case."

"I'll drive, ma'am," Sergeant Flowers said as DCI Parker
and he headed outside. To his surprise she answered, "All
right, Sergeant, but let's get a move on."

They drove in silence to Goderich both deep in thought.
Turning left at the traffic lights by McDonalds they were soon
parked on Warren Street outside Dr. Millers house. Susan
knocked on the door. It was opened by Sonja.

"Hi, Sonja." Susan said in a pleasant voice.

"Yes, what is it this time? I'm getting a little tired of all
these questions."

Sonja was wearing a low-cut t-shirt and a pair of high-top
shorts. Her long hair was loose and almost reached the middle
of her back, it hung like a cascading waterfall. The last time
Susan had interviewed Sonja she had been dressed conserva-
tively with her long hair braided in a single rope like plait. She
looked younger and more vulnerable in her shorts and t-shirt.

"We are actually looking for Deborah. Is she in?"

Sonja looked at Susan and Sergeant Flowers with a quizzical look on her face. "Deborah's not here right now. Do you mind me asking why you want to speak to her again?"

"Can we come in for a moment and maybe you could answer some questions?" Sergeant Flowers said with one foot already holding the front door open preventing Sonja from closing it.

Sonja hesitated, "Umm...yes, certainly come in, but both Deb and I have already told you everything that we know, in fact several times over. Is it entirely necessary to answer even more questions?"

Susan stepped forward and said crisply, "You do understand that this is a murder enquiry. We just have a couple more questions to ask you and then we will leave you in peace."

"Okay, then come in. My husband will be home soon, though. Maybe you would like to question him again?"

"We'll see, although it's really Isabella we want to speak to here."

"Isabella. Who on earth are you talking about?"

"We're talking about Isabella Cabello who is posing as Deborah."

"Look, I know who Deb is, but this Isabella? Please explain who it is you're talking about?"

They had entered the house and were now in the living room. Susan sat down on the sofa and patted the seat beside her for Sonja to join her.

"Come and sit down, Sonja, we need to have a long chat with you. Now please, tell us all you know about Isabella."

Sonja sat still and then it was as if all the air had gone out of a balloon. Her body slumped, and her chin dropped.

"I only ever knew her as Deb and for the first few years after she had met and cohabitated with Seb and I, everything seemed to be fine. I guess we were too busy learning how to share Seb and live together in harmony for me to be suspicious. I have to admit that I discovered her real identity completely by accident one day when I found a passport hidden at the bottom of her undie's drawer."

Sonja fidgeted in her seat and bit her fingernail before continuing to talk.

"I Googled her name, Cabello, and up popped the links to the Venezuelan drug cartel. Once I knew that she was assuming a fake identity, I watched her carefully, observing her movements. At least once a month Deb said that she had to visit an elderly aunt near Listowel. She would be gone a couple of days. Seb and I never questioned her, in fact she had us feeling sorry for this aunt who apparently lived on a farm all by herself. I did offer once to accompany her, but she declined my offer by saying that her aunt was almost a recluse and wouldn't like a stranger coming into her home. Look, we just thought that Deb had her own reasons for assuming a new identity. Maybe she just needed her own space."

"So you are telling me that you had no clue that she was involved with drug trafficking?"

"Your Constable already asked me that question and I can honestly say I had no idea that anyone in our family used drugs. I suppose my brother got into it through Juliet, but I don't think he was doing drugs before he met her and Seb and I have never, ever done drugs."

"We will have to search your house then. You won't object?"

"No, please go ahead we have nothing to hide. You will not find any illegal drugs in our home."

"Right, we will obtain a warrant and send in the sniffer dogs, but right now we need to find Deb or, to use her real name, Isabella."

"As far as I know, Deb was going shopping in London today. She left before Seb and I got up this morning, but she left us a note saying that she would be back this evening. You are welcome to wait, or I could just phone you when she gets in?"

"Okay, Sonja, I'm sorry to have disturbed you again and you have been most cooperative, particularly as I know that you are still grieving the loss of your brother. One thing I do ask of you though, is please do not let Deb know that we know her real identity.

"This woman is a known killer and could endanger your life and that of Seb's. She is ruthless and will not stop at anything. Please do not have a false sense of loyalty towards her. I cannot stress enough how dangerous she is. In fact, don't tell Seb anything as he might let the cat out of the bag."

Sonja looked horrified. "Now you're really scaring me."

"Sonja, just act normally because if you don't she'll be on to you. Here's my card, phone me the minute that she returns home."

Susan and Sergeant Flowers left shortly afterwards and drove back to Bayfield deep in thought.

THIRTY-SEVEN

R ose had just finished making the chocolate cake when the phone rang. It was Peggy Grieson. She had not spoken to Peggy for months, in fact, since that horrible day the previous summer when Rose had almost lost her life, she might have seen Peggy only a couple of times.

Peggy who used to be the Chair of the Town Hall committee, who was once terrifically involved in the village, and a pillar of the community, had become a recluse and was rarely seen in the village after the doctor's death.

On the odd occasion Rose had bumped into her she had appeared distant and almost hostile towards Rose as if she blamed her for the Doctor's demise. It was sad, though, Rose thought as Peggy and Doctor had almost been inseparable, like an old married couple.

Although both were widowers, they had found friendship with each other in the twilight of their lives. So, it was strange that Peggy should be phoning Rose.

She picked up the phone and said, "Rose, speaking."

There was a pause on the end of the line and then Peggy's

voice, "Rose, I thought that you should know that your husband was seen cavorting with that detective woman. They were outside that new restaurant and were locked in an embrace for all the world to see. It was quite shocking really."

Rose was lost for words. Tom and Susan embracing on Main Street? It seemed unlikely, but she had always known that there had been something between Susan and Tom. She had never in a million years thought of confronting Tom. It was a case of let sleeping dogs lie, but what now?"

"Umm... thank you, Peggy for drawing my attention to this. I'm sure it's nothing. I must go now." She wasn't about to engage in a conversation with such a mischief maker. There had been something rather malicious about Peggy's call that deeply disturbed Rose.

Tom returned half an hour later. He had been drinking. Rose could smell the beer on his breath.

"So, did you have a good game of golf, Tom?" Rose asked him as he sat down in the living room.

"Yes, great. We went for a quick drink afterwards to the Albion. What about your day, love? Did you have coffee with Karen?"

"Oh, yes, and the lake looked beautiful. We sat outside on the patio over looking the water. Did you meet anyone in the village?"

Rose was fishing. She wanted to believe in Tom's innocence, but still there was a little nagging doubt gnawing away in her mind.

"Oh, yes, I briefly ran into Susan as I was heading to the Albion. She was having lunch with that nice pathologist from Goderich, I can't remember his name."

"Tom, did you embrace Susan?"

There, she had said it, just blurted it out and now it was out in the open she felt better.

Tom looked aghast. He spluttered, "Embrace her as in kiss or what? Where's this coming from, Rose? Look, she ran into me, literally, and I grabbed her to stop us both from falling. That's all. What's this all about?"

Rose could see that Tom was angry. He rarely lost his temper or raised his voice.

"Hold on, Tom. Peggy Grieson took great pleasure in calling to tell me that you had been seen embracing Susan on Main Street. You know how the village can gossip and some people just love to stir the pot."

"Well, you must have believed her to even ask me if I had embraced Susan. Honestly, Rose, this sort of pettiness really is beneath you. I'm going to phone that old bat and tell her to stop spreading malicious rumours. How dare she sully my name."

"Calm down, Tom. Now I wish that I'd never told you. Look, I've made a shepherd's pie for dinner, let's have a nice glass of wine and sit down to enjoy our meal. Forget about Peggy Grieson, she's just a lonely old woman with nothing better to do than gossip."

"Okay, love, but I don't like to be the centre of mindless talk. It rattles me."

There's no smoke without fire, Rose thought as she went into the kitchen ready to serve dinner.

THIRTY-EIGHT
SATURDAY

The next day, the incident with Peggy had been forgotten and Tom and Rose prepared for their daughter's visit. It had been a month since Jessica, Rob, and the girls had visited them in Bayfield.

Today the sun was shining, and the temperature was unusually hot for early June. *It's definitely beach weather,* thought Rose as she prepared the beef for roasting.

"Tom, while I get lunch ready maybe you could take them all to the beach?"

Tom was buried behind a newspaper. He looked up as Rose was talking and said, "Um... what was that you said, love?"

"Oh, it doesn't matter, go back to your paper." Tom had selective hearing although Rose had wondered if his actual hearing was getting worse. *Another getting old delight,* she thought.

Jessica and the family arrived at eleven and the girls, Abby and Ella, rushed into the house crying out, "Grandma, Grandpa, we're getting a cat."

The girls loved Puff and Ben and dearly wanted a dog of their own, but Jessica and Rob had sensibly declined as they both worked, and it wouldn't be fair for a dog to be left alone all day.

"Oh, how exciting, darlings. When do you get your cat?"

"It's a rescue cat. Its name is Ethan. Oh Grandma, he's lovely."

"Well, darlings, I'm so happy for you both. Just remember to love him to pieces and he'll love you back."

Jessica came into the kitchen. She was looking serious.

"What's wrong, Jess?" Rose said while ushering the girls into the garden and giving them a ball to play with the dogs.

"Oh, Mom, Rob's been offered a really good job in Montreal. It's almost double his present salary. I think that we're going to move."

Rose's first reaction was purely selfish. She wouldn't get to see as much of her daughter or grandchildren if they moved. Her heart would surely break at the thought of the distance from Montreal to Bayfield, and the bearings that this would have on her relationship with her grandchildren.

But she didn't voice any of this and instead she hugged Jessica and said, "You know, love, Montreal is a great city and the girls can already speak French. It will be great. Dad and I will visit you. It's amazing news."

Rose pushed all thoughts of Montreal out of her mind and went along with making sure that their visit went well. Tom and the rest of the family headed out to the beach leaving Rose to put lunch together, but also giving her the space to process Jessica's news.

On the one hand she was thrilled for Rob's promotion and it would be exciting setting up home in Montreal, but, on the other hand, Tom and she would miss them very much.

Oh well, Rose thought, *nothing ever stays the same, change is inevitable, so we might as well embrace it.* Then she suddenly thought about Paul, Atsuko, and the new baby and them moving to London and she didn't feel quite so sad anymore.

Her peace was broken when they returned from the beach. The fresh air had worked up a good appetite in everyone and they tucked into Rose's lunch with unaccustomed gusto. Shortly after they had cleared away it was time for them to leave so that they could get back for Abby's figure skating class. Jessica and Rob hugged Rose and then the girls wanted to be hugged too.

"Come again soon, darlings. Now that summer is finally here we must take advantage of the beautiful weather."

Rose and Tom waved to them as they drove down Bayfield Terrace on their way back to London. *We won't be able to do this very often anymore,* Rose thought fleetingly as her heart gave a small jolt of regret. She loved her grandchildren so much; they would just have to make plenty of trips up to Montreal themselves to visit them.

THIRTY-NINE

Isabella was on the move. She had been since hearing from the Anderson's out at the farm in Listowel. She had to assume that her cover was blown; the shit had hit the fan and she had to get out of Ontario as quickly as possible. There was however one thing that she had to do before leaving Canada for good.

She believed in retribution and she had plans to fulfil her revenge before the days end. For Isabella Cabella had grown up in a world of dog eat dog, an eye for an eye, and a tooth for a tooth and she was tired of playing the docile third party in the Miller's little domestic ménage a-trois. Payback time not only for them, but for the pig-squealers.

Before she could seek out her revenge, a visit to London, Ontario was required. For ten years she had been meeting with one of London's biggest biker gangs supplying them with an endless stream of cocaine. They had been her biggest customers and had proved to be reliable business partners.

She was sure that the gang would be devastated to learn

that she was closing the business for a while at least, but she most certainly would not be operating again in the Listowel area. Her operation had worked primarily because her friend, Lydia, had been such a great mule.

Mind you, she had paid her handsomely and unfortunately Lydia's cover had now been blown. *C'est la vie*, she thought, *move on, it's time to re-invent myself yet again*.

Isabella had arranged to meet the biker gang leader, she had never known his real name, at the Tim Horton's next to the Costco near the 401. She wanted some assurance from him that her name would never be mentioned in any legal proceedings should their own operation be blown.

She was also willing to forgo the payment on the last haul of drugs as a courtesy call, more to soften the blow that surely would hit them when they realized that Lydia was now in custody and the Listowel operation shut down.

Isabella once again reviewed her options. She always carried two separate passports, one in the name of Deborah Nock and the other in the name of Isabella Cabella. She did, however, have a third passport under the name of Gabriela Gonzalez.

She would use this passport as likely her other aliases had been compromised. Besides, Gabriela Gonzalez was her actual birth name, her last name being that of her mother's surname. Her plan was to return to Venezuela and back to her family. It had been ten years since she had seen her mama who now lived in a secure compound in one of the safer residential districts of Caracas.

Venezuela was a beautiful country with an amazing biodiversity ranging from the Andes in the west, the Amazon to the south, and the Orinoco River Delta to the east. Isabella loved her country, but it was scary how dangerous it had become. There were murders committed every twenty minutes with more civilian deaths than there had been in Iraq during the entire war.

Corruption was rampant with hyperinflation, economic depression, poverty, and disease. Caracas itself was one of the most urbanized capitals in Latin America. Yes, Isabella most certainly would have to reinvent herself yet again and lose herself for a while in the streets of the city until everything died down.

She pulled her car up outside Tim Horton's, looked at her watch and realized that she was a good twenty minutes early for her meeting. She would pop in and get herself a cup of coffee. Unbeknown to her, Tone had followed her after he had heard from Susan that she was now their prime suspect. Through his connections with the biker gang, he had heard about the meeting planned with their leader to supposedly finalize some drug deal. This had alerted him and his surveillance team and now here he was observing the suspect walking into Tim Horton's. His job was to quietly watch her movements and contact Head Office if there appeared anything untoward.

Isabella paid for her coffee and was about to take it to go when she saw a biker looking at her from across the parking lot. At first, she thought that he was her contact, but on closer observation there was something about him that rang an alarm bell. Where had she seen him before?

She scanned through her memory. Was he from Goderich she wondered? Maybe he was one of Sonja and Seb's clients? No, he was definitely a biker. Then it came to her, she had seen this man up by the Anderson farm. Could he have been one of the drug squad surveillance team? Every instinct in her body let out warning signals. Isabella weighed up her options. She could possibly exit Tim Horton's via the side door over by the drive-thru. Waiting until the bikers back was turned away, she crept out the side of Tim Horton's and ran to where her car was parked. She drove off as fast as she could and headed down the 401. Her meeting with the biker gang leader would have to wait. She would drive back to Lake Huron and put into motion her plan for retribution.

SUSAN RECEIVED the call from Tone and listened while he described the woman he had got to know as Deb. Having confirmed that it was indeed the same person, he asked Susan what she wanted him to do.

"The trouble is, Tone, unless we catch her in the act of handing over or receiving illegal drugs, she will just flatly deny all knowledge. Keep watching her and don't let her out of your sight. Remember that we are dealing with a murderer."

Tone turned around having finished his call and couldn't see where Deb had gone. He then saw her race by in her car and he ran back to his bike and took chase.

ISABELLA WAS unaware to begin with that she was being followed. Speeding down the 401 she branched off at Wonderland Road and went north across the city until she came to Highway 22. While driving she had silently bemoaned the series of events that had led to this need to flee the country. Looking back to the events that lead to the murder of Juliet and James she felt no remorse.

Juliet had threatened to expose her having discovered

Lydia and her exchanging money and drugs that fateful evening at the couple's retreat. She could not afford to have been exposed by Juliet, besides she never held with blackmail and so when, under the pretext of wanting to talk to Juliet in the cabin, Isabella neatly silenced her. She then realized that James, her lover, would also be part of the potential blackmail scenario so he also had to go. She had no regrets at all, but she still had to deal with two more couples and then she would be able to leave Canada for good.

Looking in her car mirror Isabella noticed a motor bike in the distance. It was probably the same biker who had been following her, and he was closing the distance between them. Isabella decided to lose him. Putting her foot down she made a sharp left and then a right and then pulled into a narrow farm lane way. As expected she watched as the biker zoomed past. She then reversed and drove off in the opposite direction. *That would keep him occupied for a while*, she thought as she drove through Ailsa Craig and then towards Park Hill. Should she go to Goderich first or Bayfield? Turning the radio on Isabella tuned into the local station, 104.9 The Beach. The news was on and she just caught the tail end of one of the announcements "...one of Ontario's biggest drug busts has taken place, over 30 farms across Southwestern Ontario have been implicated in the trafficking of cocaine brought up from Mexico."

Isabella felt rage burn deep inside of her. She knew that her carefully controlled and managed ring had been busted, but somehow hearing it on the radio really brought it home to her. She pulled her car over and leant to open the glove box on the passenger's side. Inside was her revolver. It had been her father's gun. When she was eighteen he had given it to her. That was one of her fondest memories of her dad. He was shot down in broad daylight in the streets of Caracas just two weeks later. Isabella cupped the gun in her hands and then slipped it into her purse. Although she preferred killing by using the tried and tested martial arts movements she had been taught, shooting would be much quicker. She had made up her mind, she would visit Bayfield first.

FORTY

Rose and Tom had spent the afternoon clearing up after Jessica, Rob, and the girls had departed. Neither of them felt at all hungry so Rose suggested that they have a late supper when they felt hungry.

"I think that I'll take the dogs for a walk," Tom said, and Rose nodded, "Do you want to come to?"

"Not now, darling, I'm ready to just collapse with a sherry and my book. I'll see you later."

Tom grabbed the dog's leashes, gave Rose a quick kiss on her cheek, and went out of the front door. As he was walking down Bayfield Terrace he noticed a car cruising by as if looking for a house. It pulled up alongside Tom and the driver's window lowered. A pleasant looking woman smiled at Tom and said, "Hi, I'm looking for the Blair's house, could you point me in the right direction?"

Tom laughed, "Well, I've just come from there myself, it's that house over there with the white picket fence in the front," Tom pointed to his house. "I suppose it's Rose you want to see, she's there."

"Thank you, you've been most helpful." Isabella drove off and Tom continued his walk. He decided that as the dogs had been on the beach most of the afternoon and had spent further time playing ball with Abby and Ella in their garden, they probably wouldn't want a long walk. He would do a once around the block walk and be back to join Rose in the sitting room. He wondered who their visitor was and hoped that she would not be staying too long.

Rose had just sat down with a lovely glass of sherry when the doorbell rang. She reluctantly got up and opened the door to a smiling young woman.

"Oh, hi, can I help you?"

Suddenly the smile left the woman's face as she pushed Rose roughly inside the house from the lobby.

"Hey, stop that." Rose managed to say before realising that she had a pistol aimed at her chest.

"Just go into the living room, slowly, and don't try anything clever," the woman shouted.

"Who are you? What do you want?" Rose stuttered.

"Shut up, you bitch. You and your meddling husband destroyed ten years of my hard work. You should have died in that barn and been fed to the pigs."

Suddenly Rose understood to whom she was talking, and what she was talking about.

"Who are you? I thought that they'd caught the operator, that Lydia woman."

Isabella snarled, "Lydia worked for me and now thanks to you the drug ring has been broken."

"But you can start again." Rose said desperately fishing for words. If she could delay the manic woman long enough, Tom would return. *But then*, Rose thought, *if Tom returned, he would also be on the firing range from the deranged woman.*

"So, Lydia and you were friends then?"

"Yes, we've known each other for years. Stop talking bitch, I know what you're doing, you're just trying to play delay tactics. Now listen to me. This is how it will go and play out. I'm going to shoot you and then when your lovely husband returns, I'm going to shoot him too. Then, I'm going to drive to Goderich where I will repeat this same scenario with the Millers. There, now you know."

Rose began to feel very nervous. She looked around the room to see if there was anything at all that she could grab. She was just contemplating the lamp when Tom came through the door whistling a tune less tune to himself. Puff and Ben charged in and immediately started to growl and snarl at the woman.

"What the hell?" Tom shouted and that provoked another volley of barking and the dogs charged forward.

There was an almighty explosion as the air shattered and Puff let out an ear-piercing yelp. He lay bleeding on the ground. Rose screamed, and Tom felt the anger rise in his belly and gall in his throat. Before he could stop to think, he dove at the woman's legs. A second shot went off this time up to the ceiling. Tom pounded the woman on the ground. Rose had to shout out, "Tom, enough, my love, you'll kill her."

She had grabbed the gun and was now pointing it at the woman.

"Oh, Tom, Puff, look at Puff. Oh my God, he's not dead, is he?"

Puff was bleeding profusely from a bullet wound in his shoulder.

"Tom, we'll have to get him to the vets otherwise he'll surely die," Rose whispered. "Take him. I'll call Susan and I'll watch this mad woman while you take Puff to the vet. Please Tom, please."

Tom nodded and got off the floor and off the woman whom he had pinned down in a rugby tackle.

"Keep that gun pointed at her at all times, Rose. I'll phone Susan on my way to the vets. Now I'm just going to get a blanket to wrap Puff up in. Be careful, love, be really careful."

As Tom went to leave he couldn't resist letting out a sharp kick to the mad woman. "That's from Puff to you," he muttered.

Isabella groaned, and her eyes fluttered. Rose stood rooted to the spot, the pistol gripped tightly in her hand. With Tom gone it was up to her to keep watch over the woman while she waited for Susan to arrive. *Please, please be quick*, she thought, *I'm really scared of this woman.*

Ben, their beloved black Labrador, stood resolutely by her side occasionally letting out a menacing growl at Isabella who opened her eyes and glared up at Rose. She lay still and then, suddenly, like an unleashed cobra, she sprang up onto her feet, uncoiling her body in one fluid movement, and ran like a bolt of lightning, out towards the front door.

Rose was stunned and slow to react. Ben started barking crazily and charged forward after Isabella which goaded Rose into action. She yelled out, "Stop or I'll shoot," which sounded so bizarre to her own ears that had she had the luxury of time she might have laughed at the absurdity of it all.

Rose ran out the front door and got there just as Isabella was jumping into her car. A little voice inside of her said, "Go on, Rose, shoot, shoot at the car tires," but she couldn't, and Isabella had known that all along, for Rose had never in her life fired a gun.

The car raced down Bayfield Terrace towards Short Hill.

Rose ran back inside the house and picked up her phone to call Susan.

Tom, in the meantime, was half way to Zurich where the Veterinarian had his practice. As soon as he was out on the highway he had placed the call to Susan who had said that she would be on her way as soon as she had dispatched the emergency back up calls.

Puff was bleeding profusely, the blanket he was wrapped in was already soaked in blood. His breathing was shallow, and Tom feared that he might die before he even got to the vets. He pulled up outside the building.

The receptionist, on seeing the blood-soaked blanket and Puff held within, shouted for the doctor who came running out, took one look at Puff and urged Tom to follow him into the operating room.

"He's lost a lot of blood. The first thing I'm going to do is give him a blood transfusion and then clean him up. You say it's a bullet wound. Yes, yes, I can see the entry point here," the doctor had Puff up on an examination table. Tom stroked the dog gently while the doctor looked more closely at the wound.

"I'm going to give him an injection now. This will sedate him and then I'll get him hooked up to the transfusion. Look, there's no need for you to stay. I'll phone you the minute I have some news, but I do have to prepare you for the worse."

Tom looked as if he might burst into tears, but he pulled himself together and gave Puff a hug, "Hold on in there, buddy. I'll be back for you soon," he said softly and thanked the vet. He walked to his car barely noticing the blood-soaked passenger seat and drove back to Bayfield with a huge lump in his throat.

Susan arrived a few minutes later after Rose had placed her panic call. She found her friend still clutching the gun.

"Rose, give me the gun, please."

It was a small, black Beretta 42. When Susan took it from Rose the safety latch was still in place. *The poor woman wouldn't have been able to fire it even if she had tried,* Susan thought, but didn't say anything as she could see that Rose was still traumatized.

"Take a deep breath now and tell me what happened."

Rose gulped and then slowly relayed the story ending with the woman jumping in her car and driving away.

Susan had already sent out a dispatch to alert the OPP. Tom had told her that the woman had been driving a light blue Ford Escape. He could only remember partially the license plate number starting with CA and ending in 987.

Rose looked at Susan and said in a quivery voice, "So what on earth is this all about? Just who was that mad woman?"

"We thought Lydia was the murderer Rose, but it happens that she was just the drug mule for the whole operation. No, the woman you saw, her name is Deborah Nock, alias Isabella Cabellas, and she is the mastermind behind everything. Furthermore, we believe that she is also behind the two murders."

"Oh my gosh, Susan, but why did she try to kill me? If it hadn't had been for Puff and Tom intervening I would be lying dead right now."

The enormity of it all suddenly overwhelmed Rose and tears started to flow. Susan wrapped her arms around her friend and patted her back gently. "Oh, poor Rose. I don't know how you do it, but somehow you always find yourself in the thick of it. As to why she would want you dead I can only speculate.

"Probably because you and Tom blew open the whole drug

ring in Listowel. We're talking about a multimillion-dollar operation going belly-up because of your involvement."

Rose interrupted Susan, "But all we did was stop to see if we could help Lydia. We had absolutely no idea that it was a drug drop."

"Yes, I know that, but you also found Juliet's body at Ivy Cottage and to Isabella it would appear that you were snooping around just too much."

Before Susan could continue, Tom pulled up in his car and jumped out. He ran into the house crying out, "Rose, Rose, are you all right?" He rushed over to her and hugged her tightly.

"Tom, what about Puff?"

"He's in good hands, love, we'll just have to wait and see if he pulls through."

Susan had received a phone call and was intently listening.

"I have to go now folks. I'll be back, and we'll talk then." She ran out of the room, leapt into her silver Porsche, and pulled away leaving a cloud of gravel in her wake.

FORTY-ONE

Tone had lost Isabella and had conceded his defeat. He decided to continue to Goderich before heading to Bayfield where he hoped to meet up with the lovely Susan. He couldn't believe how quickly she had got under his skin. He had never believed that he would ever find true love again. His wife, who had died a horrible death from cancer, had been his childhood sweetheart. They had never had children though, which had been a deep sadness they had both born with great stoicism.

Susan was like a breath of fresh air in his otherwise sterile life. After his wife had passed away he had thrown himself into work volunteering to do undercover work infiltrating himself into the biker's world. It was extremely dangerous work, but he thought that he had nothing left to live for until he had met Susan. Was it really only a week since he had first met her?

Tone stopped off at McDonalds to grab a burger and fries. He had somehow skipped having lunch and was absolutely starving. He had just finished eating and was getting up to leave when, looking out the window, he saw a light blue Ford Escape pull up to the traffic lights. He immediately recognized the driver. It was Isabella. Tone ran out of McDonalds and jumped onto his Harley. She had turned left onto Sun Coast Drive and was headed west towards the lake. The trouble with being on a bike was that it was not easy to follow anyone as a lone biker stood out like a sore thumb on any road, but even more so in a residential area. He held back and kept his distance.

Isabella drove to the end of Sun Coast Drive and then turned left and right onto Warren Street. How many times had she driven this route back to the so-called domestic bliss of servicing that sexual pervert, Dr. Miller and indeed that sycophant, Sonja?

At first when they had all three got together it had been exciting and different and the sex had been amazing. Isabella had few sexual inhibitions, she was willing to experiment, but she had drawn the line at threesome sex. Seb Miller was a chauvinistic pig and she had begun to hate the way he had to control everything right down to their sexual encounters. No, like a cancer she would cut that part of her life out and start a-fresh.

She pulled up outside their house and parked the car in the driveway.

Inside, Sonja and Seb had just finished eating dinner. Sonja looked out of the window after she had heard a car pull up. She was shocked to see Deb in the driveway. Seb was still unaware of Deb's duplicity, but Sonja knew that she had to let Susan know that Deb, or was it Isabella, was back. She picked up her phone and quietly left the room and walked up to the front door, she drew the bolt that they had fitted a few years ago after a rash of burglaries. Walking to the rear of the house, she did the same with the back door. She then made her phone call to Susan.

Susan answered straight away, "DCI Parker speaking."

"Susan," Sonja whispered, "She's here, Deb is here, what do we do?"

Susan was extremely concerned. If Isabella had left Rose and driven straight to Goderich it meant just one thing and one thing only, retribution. She had obviously returned to settle old scores.

"Look, Sonja, I think that you and Seb might be in extreme danger. The police will be there soon, I promise. Lock all of your doors, get out of sight of the windows and hold on tight."

Seb had noticed Deb's car parked in the driveway.

"It's our Deborah back from London just in time for dinner. Did you save her some, Sonja?"

"Look, Seb, you have to know something so please, for once, listen to me. Deb is not our Deborah; her real name is Isabella and she's wanted by Interpol and here in Canada. She's a killer and is extremely dangerous."

Seb Miller looked incredulously at Sonja. "You've got to be kidding me?"

"No, I'm not. Any minute now she's going to put her key in the lock and try to come in. I've bolted both doors, but that won't hold her back for long. The police are on their way, but we have to hide or something and quickly."

Seb still looked at Sonja as if she was off her head.

"Are you really serious? This has to be some sick kind of joke?"

"No. Do I look like I'm joking?"

Just then they could hear a key in the lock turning and then the handle shake. It would not open because of the bolt.

"Quick, Seb, we need to hide. Any minute now she's going

to look through the window and see us. Come quickly, we'll go downstairs."

Their house was a split ranch style home with a fully made up basement. There was a large storage room at the bottom of the stairs which had no windows. Sonja pulled open the door and pushed Seb in, closing the door behind them.

Tone turned off his engine and pushed his bike down the road so as not to draw attention to himself. He then left it locked up in the driveway of a house four doors up from the Millers. Removing his leather jacket and helmet and storing them under his bike, he then walked casually along the sidewalk until he was in plain view of the Millers house. There he observed Isabella trying to open the front door. He pulled out his iPhone and placed a call to Susan.

"Susan, it's me," Tone said in a hushed voice, "I'm outside the Millers house, Isabella is here trying to get inside."

Susan already knew this because she had just spoken to Sonja.

"Thank God you're over there, Tone. Look, the police are on their way and I'm in the car driving as we speak. Whatever you do be careful. We're dealing with a killer who has shown no remorse. As far as we know she is not armed, but she has extensive training in the martial arts and knows how to kill.

"I've already told the Millers to lock up their doors and hide, but my guess is that will only delay her entering the house by minutes. She'll probably break a window or something."

As Susan spoke Tone could hear glass shattering. "I must go, Susan." He put his phone away and ran to the Millers house.

Sure enough the side windowpane was smashed. He was undecided, should he wait for the back up team or go in after her himself? Sonja's piercing scream made the decision for him. He jumped through the broken window and stood there for a second just listening. Hearing voices coming from the basement, he ran quickly and found the door at the bottom of the stairs ajar.

What greeted him was like a set tableau with the main characters poised like in a play. Seb Miller was lying on the floor, Sonja bent over him and Isabella posed in a karate stance just ready to attack. Time stood still. Isabella was about to lunge forward and strike when Sonja charged like a wild beast. She hit Isabella with all her might and as she did so, in the split second that it took, Tone rushed forward and grabbed her by her neck. Isabella kicked out and he almost lost his grip before Sonja grabbed Isabella's arms and pinned them down while Tone pushed her to the floor.

"The police are on their way," Tone said to Sonja who had gone back to where Seb lay flat on the floor with his head at an unnatural angle.

"What happened?" Tone asked gently while nodding in Seb's direction.

"She was as quick as lightning. Before we knew it, the door opened, and Deb grabbed Seb by the neck, put her foot on his back, gave a quick twist, and that was it, his life was over, just like that."

Here Sonja wrung her hands together in a twisting action, "My God, it was like watching my mother twisting the chicken's necks for our dinner. I'm afraid that he's dead." Her voice choked up and she began to sob, deep heart rending sobs.

"You know he was a good man although he had an insatiable desire for sex. Nobody should be murdered for wanting that, should they? Oh, and he was so good in bed."

Tone could see that Sonja was in shock and as a result was

babbling on too much. He would have comforted her if it wasn't for the fact that he daren't

move from where he had pinned Isabella down.

Soon they could hear the police sirens getting louder and louder as they drew closer. The next thing they heard was the thunder of footsteps thudding down the stairs and soon they were surrounded by half a dozen police officers. Finally, Tone could release his charge to the authorities.

Isabella was like a wild animal kicking and scratching as the officer attempted to zip the plastic handcuffs around her wrists and take her into custody. She shouted and swore and generally cursed everybody and everything in her sight. Isabella was determined to not go quietly. She would employ the best lawyer in the province to take on her case. This was not the end for her, only the beginning of just another fight.

Susan arrived shortly afterwards. She rushed into the building and ran down the stairs.

"Tone, are you alright?"

She wanted to hug and kiss him when she saw him standing there, but it would have not been at all professional in front of all the officers. Instead she quietly said to him, "Can you come over to my place tonight?"

He smiled his sexy, lopsided grin and whispered, "Sure, I can't wait."

FORTY-TWO

Rose and Tom waited anxiously by the phone for the call from the vet's office. Finally, when it came, they were both almost too nervous to take it. Tom picked up the phone. "Tom Blair."

"Ah, yes, Mr. Blair. We are calling about Puff. Look, we've managed to stabilize him and given him a blood transfusion, but I'm afraid you're going to have to take him to Guelph. His shoulder will require surgery to remove the bullet, it's just too deeply embedded for me to pull it out. When can you take him? The sooner the better."

Tom looked at his watch and then at his wife's worried face. Rose looked haggard with exhaustion. Losing Puff would just devastate her, particularly as she had rescued him after her best friend, Mary had died, and the poor dog had been orphaned several years ago.

"We'll take him now if the hospital will still be open. We won't get there before nine o'clock though."

"They're open all night long." the doctor said. "We'll have him ready for you, say, in twenty minutes? Make sure that you have a clean towel or sheet on the back seat of your car. We want to minimize any infection."

Tom put the phone down and told Rose to pack an overnight bag.

"We might have to book into a motel, love."

"What about Ben?"

"Phone Lynda and see if she could look after him, love, but be quick we must get on the road soon."

Lynda agreed to come over and pick up Ben, and soon Rose and Tom were on the road. Twenty minutes later Tom carried a very sedated Puff and laid him gently on the sheet at the back of the car. Rose stroked Puff and then covered him with a warm blanket. They drove off to Highway 4 and then onto Seaforth, heading towards the 401.

Arriving at Guelph Animal Hospital two hours later, Rose and Tom were greeted by a veterinarian assistant who wheeled out a trolley for Puff to lay on. They followed the trolley into the hospital where a very stern looking man, presumably the surgeon, dressed in green scrubs, approached them.

"A bullet wound, eh? We'll take it from here. Go and get some rest and please do not call us before seven in the morning."

Tom looked at Rose and bit his tongue. He sighed and then conceded to the surgeon. The man's manner was gruff, but hopefully he knew his stuff. They would check into a motel and leave their beloved dog in the hands of professionals.

FORTY-THREE

SUNDAY

I t was a long, long night. Several times Rose and Tom had to resist the urge to phone the hospital. By seven o'clock they could not wait a second longer. This time Rose took the phone.

"Guelph Animal Hospital, how can I help you? "Came the response from the receptionist.

"This is Rose Blair, Puff's owner. How is he?"

"I'll have to check and see. You said, Puff? Hold on please."

Rose held her breath while they waited for the nurse to return.

"Puff is doing just fine. They were able to remove all of the bullet and fortunately none of his vital organs were damaged by the trauma. He has come around from his anaesthetic and he's even eaten a big bowl of food this morning and more importantly, he's gone to the washroom. You may pick him up whenever you're ready."

"Oh, thank you, thank you."

Rose smiled at Tom and Tom hugged her.

"He's going to be okay, Tom, he's okay."

A SNEAK PEEK AT MURDER AT WINDMILL LAKE!

Tom stood by the water's edge looking out across the glistening lake. It seemed incredible to think that someone had created the man-made lake and then constructed the majestic windmill which was now perched proudly upon a wooden platform near the side of the lake. *Who had been the previous owner,* Tom thought as he watched a gangly heron swoop and skim across the water in one fluid movement, long beak in and out and then back in the air again, fish in its mouth.

There were a few paddle boarders out on the lake, but most of the activity was centered upon wakeboarding. Indeed, it had been Abby and Ella, his granddaughters' idea to spend the afternoon at the eco-park. The previous summer they had attended a wakeboard and art camp and had loved every minute of it. When Tom and Rose's daughter, Jessica, had asked if Abby and Ella could spend a couple of weeks with them, Rose had immediately registered the girls for an afternoon at Windmill Lake. Judging by the squeals of delight he could hear they were having a great time although it would soon be time to head back home.

Tom looked at his watch and then turned towards the windmill. It was then that he remembered the original owner's name, Frank de Jong. He had read about the amazing project which had taken almost twenty years to complete and had finally opened in 1989. Apparently, Frank de Jong had modelled the design of the windmill based on a mill that was located in Harlingen in Holland. His grandfather had worked as the master miller at this mill. It had taken the whole of one summer just to build the foundations and erect the concrete pillars which would support the whole structure. The actual windmill itself would end up being over ninety-five feet tall and was built from trees grown on the de Jong's own property woodland.

Walking towards where Rose was sitting watching the girls wakeboard, Tom almost bumped into a man who appeared to be in a tremendous hurry. He was carrying a black, tubular fishing rod case and was wearing, rather incongruously for the time of year, a full-length Barber jacket.

"Oh, I'm sorry," Tom said amicably. "I didn't see you."

"*Potverdore*," the man hissed as he pushed past Tom and continued walking briskly towards the car park.

What a rude man, Tom thought as he watched him in the distance get in a car and begin to drive away. *Oh, well, it takes all sorts*, he mused. Tom was about to join Rose when he stopped suddenly and looked back towards the windmill. What was it that had caught his attention back there? He retraced his steps to where the windmill sat on its concrete pillars. Looking up and around Tom scanned the area with his sharp eyes. It was then that he saw a pair of legs partially concealed from view protruding from beneath the platform.

With some trepidation, Tom walked over to the structure and peered underneath the deck. What he saw was not a pretty sight. A man lay sprawled on the ground with what looked like half his head blown off. Blood and particles of brain matter were splattered everywhere. Tom felt his stomach lurch and before he could prevent himself, he had vomited violently into the grass. Wiping his mouth with the back of his hand, he groped in his pocket for his phone and punched in 911.

ALSO BY JUDY KEIGHTLEY

ABOUT THE AUTHOR

Over the past thirty years Judy has written twenty novellas, various collections of poetry and a number of plays. Judy wrote her first full length novel in 2013 and developed it into a series called the Rose Blair Murder Mysteries all set in the sleepy village of Bayfield on the beautiful shores of Lake Huron in Ontario, Canada.

Judy and her husband reside in Bayfield with their beloved dog Susie and cat Thomas and enjoy visits from their children and grandchildren.

After retiring Judy and her husband took on a new challenge in their lives. Purchasing land on the outskirts of Bayfield they have planted a six acre vineyard and are in the process of designing and building a boutique winery.

Life is beautiful and sweet. I feel so very blessed with all my wonderful family and friends who continually surround me with their love.

FIND OUT MORE!

Find Cozy House Press online to read more great cozy mysteries!

www.cozyhousepress.com

COZY HOUSE PRESS
MAKE A DATE WITH MURDER